THE CHERRY VALLEY MIDDLE SCHOOL

DEAR KNOW-IT-ALL

★ ★ ★

Texting 1, 2, 3

by RACHEL WISE

Simon Spotlight
New York London Toronto Sydney New Delhi

This book is a work of fiction. Any references to historical events, real people, or real places are used fictitiously. Other names, characters, places, and events are products of the author's imagination, and any resemblance to actual events or places or persons, living or dead, is entirely coincidental.

SIMON SPOTLIGHT
An imprint of Simon & Schuster Children's Publishing Division
1230 Avenue of the Americas, New York, New York 10020
Copyright © 2013 by Simon & Schuster, Inc. All rights reserved, including the right of reproduction in whole or in part in any form.
SIMON SPOTLIGHT and colophon are registered trademarks of Simon & Schuster, Inc.
Text by Veera Hiranandani
Designed by Bob Steimle

For information about special discounts for bulk purchases, please contact Simon & Schuster Special Sales at 1-866-506-1949 or business@simonandschuster.com.
Manufactured in the United States of America 0613 OFF
First Edition 10 9 8 7 6 5 4 3 2 1
ISBN 978-1-4424-7519-9 (pbk)
ISBN 978-1-4424-7520-5 (hc)
ISBN 978-1-4424-7521-2 (eBook)
Library of Congress Control Number 2013939384

Chapter 1

BREAKING NEWS: YOUNG GIRL MELTS ON SIDEWALK DURING RECORD HEAT

★ ★ ★

It's hot. Right now as I sit on my front steps waiting for my BFF, Hailey Jones, and her mom to take us to the air-conditioned mall on the third day of an awful heat wave, it's the kind of hot that makes me wonder if I could actually dissolve into a unrecognizable blob of goo by the time Hailey gets here. *Breaking News: Young Girl Melts on Sidewalk During Record Heat* is what I'm thinking.

It's also the kind of hot that makes me wish for a chill in the air and sweaters and, believe it or not, school. School just goes with fall. School also goes with seeing my forever and ever crush, Michael Lawrence, every day. I haven't seen him since the town's Fourth of July fireworks display, which was awesome. Hailey, Michael and his friend Frank, and I all went together. I couldn't really call it a double date since Hailey says she doesn't have a crush on Frank, but he definitely has a crush on her and maybe one of these days Hailey will like him back. Hailey says he's a really nice guy, but his hair is too dark and his ears are too big for her taste. I think she's actually afraid to like someone she knows has a big crush on her. But that secret's just between me and me.

Anyway, the way we decided to go together is because we ran into each other at the movies the night before and all decided to go together to the fireworks, so it was a group decision. I don't think that officially counts as a double date. Still, Michael and I shared a cotton candy and sat pretty close while the fireworks were happening. I couldn't tell what was making my heart beat faster—the fireworks or sitting on a picnic blanket in the dark with Michael Lawrence!

Since then though, I haven't seen him, like, at all. It's been more than six weeks. He went to baseball camp, Hailey went to soccer camp, and I went to journalism camp. Hailey couldn't understand why I'd want to spend any part of my summer writing. But journalism is my passion, just like soccer and sports in general are hers. I got to brush up on my reporting skills and learned lots of cool stuff about being a reporter. One thing I learned is that I should finish the story before I think of the headline, which is hard for me. I love headlines. *Martone Believes Life Is a Series of Headlines.* So I guess I need to have a little more patience when it comes to putting my stamp on the story.

The only thing that bums me out about the start of school is that I've finished my tenure as Dear Know-It-All, the anonymous (I think!) advice columnist. It was a year-long gig, and since I did it all last year, my time is up. I can't imagine not doing it, but I guess I'll have more time to focus on the other writing I do for the paper. I also did NOT get to be editor in chief this year. I was hoping I would, but instead Jessica Kelly won the crown. Mr. Trigg said that I would make a great editor in chief and was one of the best reporters the *Voice* had ever had, but I still needed a little more experience under my belt. Jessica has been on the paper a year longer than I have, is super-organized, and a little bossy, which is maybe kind of how you need to be as editor in chief. So I get why Mr. Trigg chose her. It is an all-consuming job. I have to admit I was a little nervous about having that much responsibility, but I'm also disappointed because I was really up for the challenge. But Mr. Trigg said, "Ms. Martone, there's still plenty of time to see great things from you," so I guess I just need to wait.

I've been obsessing about who the new Know-It-All will be all summer, but I guess I'll never know since it's top secret. I managed never to blow my cover, as far as I know. That wasn't an easy job, but I really grew to love it and found that every time I had to give advice to someone else, I learned something new about myself. Still, it was a lot of stress. Maybe it will be good to focus on other things now. Like not melting.

Finally, just in the nick of time, Hailey's white

car pulled up. The sun glared on it so brightly, I had to shield my eyes just to look at it. I was sweating after walking the twenty feet to the car.

"Ugh, I'm surprised I didn't melt!" I said, slumping down into the backseat. The AC was blasting in the car. "It feels so good in here."

"I know," Hailey said from the front. "You have AC in your house, though, don't you?"

"Yeah, but my mom is always turning it off when we're not in the house."

"Us too," Hailey's mom said. "It costs a fortune!"

"Well, at least walking around the ice-cold mall is free," Hailey said. "Unless you buy stuff."

"And speaking of buying stuff, my mom gave me some money for a back-to-school outfit," I said, holding up my shoulder bag as if Hailey could see the money inside.

"I did the same for Hailey," Mrs. Jones said. "I used to love getting together the perfect back-to-school outfit. It would take me weeks," she added dreamily.

"Yeah, well, I just want to be cool and comfortable," Hailey said, rolling her eyes, ever practical.

She wasn't one to fuss over her clothes unless a boy was involved.

I just nodded, but secretly I wanted to get the cutest outfit I could possibly find for Michael. Since he hadn't seen me in a while, it was a chance to wow him a little bit. It's not that I wanted to look different, just a little new, I guess. I should have asked my older sister, Allie, for some advice. She always looks great.

For the first half hour at the mall, Hailey and I walked around sipping slushies and letting the frozen air sink into our bones. Once we felt refreshed, we headed over to our favorite store to check out the latest trends.

"I don't know," Hailey said as I tried on a red tank top with ruffles down the front. "It's not really you."

"Yeah, but what if I wanted to try out a new look?" I said, looking past her in the mirror and flipping my hair from side to side. I knew it was a little much, but I felt like taking a risk.

"I think what you're looking for is the You-Only-Better top, not the Who-Are-You?

top, which is what *that* is," she said, pointing at me. Then she held up a blousy white cotton shirt.

"Nah, kind of boring," I said, waving the white shirt away. I already had a few blouses like it.

"What about this one?" Hailey said, and held up a purple tunic-style tee with a really cool green design embroidered on the front.

"Hmmm," I said. "It would look nice with those leggings." I pointed to a simple black pair. I grabbed it from Hailey and tried it on. It was supercute, and the green embroidery highlighted my eyes.

"Perfect! You only better," Hailey said.

"Why not just me? Why the better part?" I asked.

"I'm just kidding with you, beauty queen," Hailey said, grinning. She went and tried on a white T-shirt, the kind that she had a million of.

"It looks good," I said, but didn't she want to punch it up? "But maybe go for something a little different."

"Come on. It's comfortable," Hailey whined.

I looked around quickly and grabbed a plain turquoise tank top. The color would look fantastic on her, and it wasn't frilly or anything.

"At least another color. White's a little boring."

"Okay, okay," she said, and disappeared into the dressing room with the tank top. She came out looking amazing. That was the thing with Hailey. It didn't take much for her to look great.

"See, it makes you look even tanner! And those white capris look perfect with it."

Hailey was looking in the mirror, a big smile spreading across her face.

"Okay, you win," she said.

We also bought new earrings—dangly silver and green beaded ones for me, turquoise studs for her—and clear lip gloss. Mom was really strict about wearing makeup or anything, but clear lip gloss was okay with her. We were ready for the first day of school, which was now one week away!

When I came home, the house felt nice and cool since my mother and Allie were home and the AC had been blasting for a while. I went into the kitchen and got a peach and sat at the counter. One of my favorite things about summer was peaches. I ate at least one a day. I took a big bite, and the juice dribbled down my chin.

My mom came into the kitchen and handed me a napkin.

"Thanks," I said, and wiped my mouth.

"Did you see my note that Mr. Trigg called?" Mom said.

I looked at the phone. There was a pink sticky note on it. I squinted my eyes. *Sam! Mr. Trigg called. Call him back. 555-1873.*

"Now I do," I said. "Huh. I wonder why he called." My mind started to race. Could there be an issue with Jessica Kelly? Maybe she bailed on the editor in chief post. A flippy feeling started to take over my stomach. Would that be a good thing? Was I really ready for that kind of responsibility?

"Sam?" my mom said in a worried tone. "Are you okay?"

"Uh, yeah," I said, snapping back into reality. "I should call him back." I got up, threw my peach pit away, and took the phone into the den.

I paused for a moment before dialing. Then I took a deep breath and went for it.

"Hello?" said Mr. Trigg's peppy British-accented voice. I have to admit I missed it.

"Hi, Mr. Trigg. This is Sam. . . ." I paused. "Martone?" I said a little unsteadily.

"Ms. Martone! How has your summer been? Brilliant, I hope?" he chirped at me.

"Yes, um, brilliant," I said back cautiously.

"Well, I have a little business to discuss with you," he said. I could tell there was an edge of excitement in his voice, but then again, there was always an edge of excitement in his voice.

"I would like you to have another go at the column," he said.

Did he mean what I think he meant? "The Dear Know-It-All column?" I asked tentatively.

"No, the lunch menu column. Of course the Know-It-All column!"

"Oh," I said, my head spinning with confusion.

"You don't sound happy." Mr. Trigg sounded a bit disappointed.

"No, I'm . . ." I paused. I couldn't believe it,

actually. "I'm thrilled! And surprised. Isn't it just a one-year thing?" I asked.

"Ms. Martone, the great thing about being the newspaper advisor is that I get to make the rules. You got the best responses last year that any Know-It-All has ever had. The position is yours again, if you'll have it."

My face flushed. "Wow, I don't know what to say."

"Say you'll do it!" Mr. Trigg cleared his throat. "I mean, if you feel you're up for it. Same deal as last year—top secret. And if for some reason you say yes now and change your mind, I need to know in the next day or two."

It did mean the stress again and adding more to my workload, but it was one of the coolest things I've done in my short career as a writer. How could I not do it? I just hoped I could keep it a secret from Hailey, Michael, and Allie for one more year.

"Of course I'll do it!" I declared.

"Excellent!" Mr. Trigg said. "We have a staff meeting on the first day of school. Three p.m. sharp. I'll see you then."

I said good-bye and hung up. My face still felt

warm. It was a really nice ego boost to be asked again. I had to tell someone the good news. I was bursting! Luckily, my mom was allowed to know my secret . . . again.

"Mom," I called. She didn't answer, and I didn't want Allie to wonder why I was yelling. I found her in the kitchen where I'd left her. She was standing up eating a peach and reading the paper. I glanced around to make sure Allie wasn't anywhere.

"I'm doing it again," I whispered in a low conspiratorial voice.

My mom lowered the paper and put her peach down on a napkin in front of her. "Doing what?" she whispered back.

"I'm going to be Dear Know-It-All again. Mr. Trigg said I got the best responses from any other Know-It-All and he wants me to do another year." This time I wasn't so quiet.

"That's great!" Mom said. "You must be proud of yourself."

I nodded, beaming. Then I heard another voice in the kitchen.

"Why should she be proud of herself?" Allie called from the hallway.

"Because . . . ," Mom said, and looked at me helplessly.

"Because Mr. Trigg called and said he wants me to do even more stories for the paper this year!" I blurted out. I saw my mom let out a breath.

Allie came padding barefoot in the kitchen. She had her hair up in a towel and a green facial mask covering her face. "Oh, big deal," she said, and then turned on her heel and walked out. Phew.

One more year of being Dear Know-It-All—I hoped I could do it!

Chapter 2

FIRST DAY OF SCHOOL STARTS INSOMNIA EPIDEMIC

★ ★ ★

It was seven a.m. I sat in the kitchen having been dressed in my new tunic, leggings, and earrings since six a.m. I can never sleep the morning of the first day of school. My eyes bounced open at five a.m. and it was still dark out. I lay in bed hoping to fall asleep again and started thinking about how I was going to feel seeing Michael and if we were going to work on a story together for the first issue of the *Voice* and if my hair would behave today and what the cafeteria would have for lunch and if Hailey would wear her new tank top and if I would like my new teachers and if Mr. Trigg would still have his lucky scarf and what my first Dear Know-It-All question would be about. That's all.

So I decided that getting up would stop the roar of thoughts streaming through my brain. I took a shower and carefully blow-dried my hair. Then I got dressed, got all my school supplies together, ate a big bowl of cornflakes and two bananas, because I'm tall and if I don't eat constantly I wither like a plant without water.

"You're the early bird this morning," Mom said, coming in to make her coffee.

"Yeah, woke up at five a.m. Nerves, I guess," I said, sipping my orange juice.

"You know, the same thing happened to me this morning," Mom said with a yawn. "Maybe your nerves are rubbing off on me." She filled the coffee carafe with water. "I'm sure you'll settle down once you get there and see that it's the same old Cherry Valley."

"I hope so," I said.

Allie stumbled in, still in her pajamas.

"Can I have some coffee?" she asked, looking a bit like an insane asylum escapee. Her hair was in a couple of big rollers on the top of her head. She was wearing mismatched p.j.'s, and she had bags under her eyes. "I don't know what happened, but I tossed and turned all night!"

This was getting a little strange. ***First Day of School Starts Insomnia Epidemic!*** Maybe a fairy sprinkled nonsleeping dust on all of us last night.

"Just a little coffee," Mom said, pouring her half a cup. "You better get going, Allie. Don't want to be late on the first day of school!"

"Yeah, yeah," Allie said, grabbing the coffee and shuffling back to her room.

Once I had my orange juice, I was feeling more energized and got to school early. School looked the same. It even smelled the same—slightly dusty attic mixed with floor cleaner. I went to my new locker and opened it up. Luckily, I got it open *and* it wasn't covered with tons of partially torn-off stickers.

"Double good," I said out loud to no one in particular.

"What's so double good about it?" said a voice. A male voice. A Michael Lawrence voice. I looked up and there he was, staring at me with his tan and his bright blue eyes. He seemed a little taller and definitely cuter, if that was even possible.

"Well . . . it's clean—my locker, I mean," I said, trying to smile and act like I wasn't nervous. Why was I suddenly so nervous around Michael? Yes, I still had a major crush on him, but I've also known him since kindergarten. Something about not seeing him for more than a month had rattled me. "That's why it's good."

"Hmmm," he said, sticking his head into my locker. "Good and clean."

"Thanks for the inspection," I said.

"So, Paste, how was the rest of your summer? You look great. I like your shirt."

Even though he still used my childhood nickname from when I ate paste in kindergarten, I liked the compliment.

"Oh, this old thing?" I said, looking down at my shirt, even though, of course, I knew what it looked like.

"Yeah, that old thing. Never seen you wear it before. You sure it's old?" he asked. Now I was starting to feel even more flustered. He actually knew my clothes well enough to know what was new and what was old?

"Uh," I said. *Oh great*, I thought. **Girl Blows It in First Conversation** was the headline in my brain.

"So how was the rest of your summer?" Michael asked, leaning against the locker next to mine.

"It was great. I loved journalism camp. Learned some supercool things that I will talk your ear off about when we do our next story," I said really fast, and then I wished I could shove the words back in my mouth. Even though we had worked on most of our stories together last year, who says we were going to this year?

"Would love to hear about it," Michael said, and he seemed to mean it.

"And I'm really psyched that I'm going to be—" and then I stopped. Did I have sudden amnesia? Did I really just almost tell Michael about the Dear Know-It-All column? I needed more sleep.

"Going to be what?" Michael asked, leaning in, curiosity piqued by my abrupt silence.

"Going to be working on the paper with you

again!" I said extra cheerfully.

"Cool. Yeah, me too," Michael said, and smiled. "Well, gotta go. Looking good, Pasty. See you at the meeting," he called as he walked off. I watched him move down the hallway and get swallowed up by all the students now swarming around their lockers.

"Yay! Our lockers are close again!" Hailey said as she walked up to a locker four down from mine.

"Yay," I said.

"Oh, you can do better than that," she said. She was wearing the tank top and white capris and looked pretty and tan and a lot better rested than I did.

"Sorry. I'm excited. I woke up so early this morning and couldn't go back to sleep, and then I think I just made a total fool of myself with Michael."

"I'm sure you didn't and, anyway, you look great, so if you did, you did it looking fab."

Frank walked by. "Hi, Hailey," he said.

"Hi, Frank," she said, and waved.

"Hi, Frank," I said, pretending to be annoyed that he didn't say hi to me.

"Oh, sorry. Hi, Sam. Didn't see you there," he said sheepishly, and then hurried off.

"He's so in love with you, he didn't even notice me!" I said, and punched her lightly in the shoulder.

"He is not," Hailey said, and punched me back, hard.

"Ow! I didn't punch you that hard," I said, and rubbed my shoulder.

"Ha! Guess I don't know my own strength," she said. "Hmmm. Frank. I don't know . . . maybe if he grew his hair longer to cover his ears? And his hair is a little too dark for my taste."

I just rolled my eyes. "What are we going to do with you?" I said. Hailey just smiled and shrugged. Frank was really cute. I honestly didn't understand why she didn't like him, but if I said that to her, she'd probably tell me if I thought he was so cute, why didn't I go for it with Frank, so I kept my mouth shut as we walked to class.

My classes went by slowly, and I almost fell

asleep in math, which wasn't like me at all. Normally, on the first day of school I'm pretty energized, and we were definitely going to learn some cool stuff in earthonomics and language arts. All my teachers seemed pretty decent, except for maybe Mrs. Fuller, my science teacher, who was known to be kind of boring and give tons of homework. But I was off today. Finally the last bell rang. I headed over to the *Voice* office, and there was Mr. Trigg with his scarf and his teapot, except for one thing that was totally different. He sported a mustache and a little goatee! That woke me right up.

I sat down, instinctively putting my backpack on the chair next to me to save it for Michael, and stared at Mr. Trigg. He was gathering up some papers on his desk. I couldn't decide if he actually looked kind of cute or a little bit scary, but it was thrilling that he looked so different, maybe even a little thinner too. A lot of other kids were there already. I saw Jessica Kelly sitting in the front, back straight as an arrow, a notebook pressed against her chest. She kept turning and glancing at the people who came in and then turning back, not smiling at anyone. Something about her rubbed me the wrong way. I missed Susannah, the old editor in chief. She was always smiling and really nice.

Michael came in at the last second, breathless. Some things never change.

"Made it!" he said, and plopped down. I saw him look at Mr. Trigg, and his eyes grew wide. He looked at me and motioned with his head over at Trigger.

"Trigger's got a new look," he whispered in my ear. I thanked Mr. Trigg silently, since his new look gave Michael a reason to whisper in my ear.

I nodded and smiled. "I think it works on him," I whispered back. Before Michael had a chance to respond, Mr. Trigg clapped his hands for quiet.

"Welcome back, journos! I hope your summers were eventful and inspiring," he announced. People quieted down. "And that you didn't forget everything you learned last year."

A few bits of laughter sounded around the room. "I'd like to welcome all the new *Voice* staffers." He swept his hand over to some of the newbies that had joined this year. "And I'm excited to congratulate the brilliant Jessica Kelly, our new editor in chief. I know this paper will thrive under her leadership."

People clapped, and Jessica turned to face the crowd and gave a stiff smile, holding tight to her notebook.

"What do you think of her?" I whispered to Michael, but before he could answer, Mr. Trigg started talking again.

"So, let's get down to business. We will cover many of the same areas as last year—sports, arts, investigative stories, human interest, and of course the Know-It-All column." A few people cheered. I prayed I wasn't blushing.

"I wonder who it is," Michael whispered. "Never found out who it was last year even though I totally tried. Hope this year's Know-It-All is as good."

I just nodded. I was speechless. Michael had *tried* to find out who Dear Know-It-All was? *Student Reporter Faints During First Newspaper Meeting.*

"But one thing that Jessica and I have talked

about is covering some of the smaller stories that affect our everyday lives. So I'd love to do something on the subject of texting," he said, and looked around.

Texting? Really? A whole story on it? It was like doing an investigative story on e-mail or using the phone. Where was the story?

"I'm sure you've all heard about the new rule here at school, since texting has only become an increasing distraction during the school day."

There were many nods. We had all gotten notices before the year started that if we were caught texting even once during the school day, we would get a detention. It was the same in the high school, and I'd had to listen to Allie rant and rave about it. It did seem harsh. As for me, I usually didn't text during the day and never during class, but I didn't see why people couldn't in between classes. It was just how our generation communicated. I wondered if it was Mr. Trigg or Jessica who'd come up with this story idea.

"This seems like a job for our dynamic duo, Ms. Martone and Mr. Lawrence," Mr. Trigg said.

Whoa. Now I really wasn't sure about the story. I raised my hand. One thing I learned at camp was to not be afraid to take risks. But this didn't seem like it fell into that category.

"Yes, Ms. Martone?" Mr. Trigg said.

"I'm just not sure this is the best story to do for the first paper. This issue has been there for a while and it's not going away, so maybe we should wait on it. Don't we want to do something more, well, groundbreaking to kick off our year?"

Jessica turned to me and spoke. "According to the *New York Times*, American teenagers send and receive an average of eighty texts per day. I'm sure a lot of people would like to know how this new rule will affect our community. What could be more current?" Jessica said.

I didn't really know what to say. How could I compete with *New York Times* stats?

"I agree it's current," Michael said. "But is it worthy of a lead story?" I was thankful he was on my side.

"Well, that's up to you guys. If you'd rather not take it on, we can find someone else." Even when Mr. Trigg was pushing us a bit, he sounded calm and jolly. I was just thinking that maybe Kate Bigley, one of the newer writers, would want to do the story, since she liked trendy, lighter pieces. I looked at her. She was sitting in front, wearing a really cute light blue beaded tee and skinny jeans. Her hair was shiny and perfect, and I would totally kind of hate her if she weren't so nice and fun. When she first moved here earlier in the year from England with her adorable English accent, Mr. Trigg had put her on a story with Michael. I'd thought my status not only as Michael's writing partner but also as the ace investigative reporter at the *Voice* was about to be lowered a few notches. It turned out she was more interested in covering fashion/celebrity pieces and had no desire to take my place, so to speak. So it had all worked out.

"No, no, I think we can do it," Michael said, and looked at me questioningly.

"Yeah, we're on it," I said. I didn't want to get split up from Michael again. At this point, we were so used to working together, it was just easier. And, of course, I wanted to work with him. After the meeting, Michael and I walked quickly down the hall to find a quiet place where we could talk.

"Hey, Paste, glad we're doing a story together, even if it's kind of lame. What's the big deal?" Michael finally said when we were alone. "Our parents passed notes during class. We text. It's a sign of the times."

"I know," I said. "But it seems like we were outvoted by Jessica Kelly."

"Yeah, she seems a little . . . ," Michael started, and paused.

"Uptight?" I said.

"Yeah, but she's probably really nervous," he said.

"You're probably right," I said. I hadn't really thought of it that way. It must be a little scary being the editor in chief of the school paper. I would be nervous too. But still, I wasn't so sure about her or our next assignment. Maybe all I needed was a little more sleep.

Chapter 3

SECRET ADVICE COLUMNIST'S COVER IS BLOWN!

★　★　★

Sleep I got. About ten hours' worth. I came home and crashed early. But the texting story didn't seem more exciting to me in the morning, and neither did a year of Jessica Kelly. At least I didn't have to deal with her for the Dear Know-It-All column. That was just between me and Mr. Trigg. I hoped there would already be some letters waiting for me today.

I was much more awake and into my classes, so the day flew by. After school, I rushed over to the *Voice* office first thing and gave my secret knock. Mr. Trigg didn't answer. I poked my head in and no one was there. I walked in quietly and opened up my secret mailbox with my special key, hoping no one would come in. I grabbed the letters out and stuffed them in a zippered pocket in my bag. Just as I was closing up my bag, the door opened. *Secret Advice Columnist's Cover Is Blown!* I quickly moved away from the mailbox and slung my bag over my shoulder.

"Hi, Sam," said Jessica. "What are you doing here?"

I wondered if she could see my heart pounding through my shirt.

"Oh, hi!" I said a little too loudly. "Just looking for Mr. Trigg."

"Back there?" Jessica asked suspiciously, since I was still in the back of the room.

"Well, um, I also needed some . . . printer paper," I said, because I was standing near a shelf that had some on it.

"We're not supposed to use the printer paper from here unless it's for the *Voice*," she said, still not cracking a smile.

"Yeah, no, I know. It is for the *Voice*, for something I needed to print out, but I can do it later,"

I said, hoping she wouldn't realize I was barely making sense.

She just nodded slowly. "Okay . . . well, Mr. Trigg has a faculty meeting. I can help you," she said, her arms crossed, just seeming, well, tense. Who did she think she was anyway—knowing Mr. Trigg's schedule and assuming she could help me? Being the editor in chief didn't mean she was a stand-in for the faculty advisor. And it certainly didn't mean she could be all bossy like she owned the place.

"Oh, that's okay. I'll try to catch him tomorrow." I walked quickly to the door. "See ya," I called as I left, hoping I sounded cheerful instead of annoyed. Wow, that was close. *What was she doing in the office, anyway?* I wondered. Usually, we all worked on our stories at home until they were ready to download in the template online. Then we tweaked everything the last couple of days in the office, and bam, the *Voice* was ready to publish. The process was even faster since we published it online now. I was going to have to be careful with Jessica hiding out in the office. Maybe I'd have to pick up my letters early in the morning.

I got home, yelled hello to Mom, and immediately locked myself in my room before Allie could even notice I was home. The texting article wasn't rocking my world and Jessica was really getting on my nerves, but at least the Dear Know-It-All column was something I could savor. Thank goodness Mr. Trigg had asked me to do it again.

I already had three letters and it was only the second day of school. Dear Know-It-All was as popular as ever! I sat on my bed cross-legged and opened the first one. It was written on wrinkled notebook paper and stuffed in a regular white envelope.

Dear Know-It-All, my feet hurt all the time. I think my toes are uneven and no matter what brand of shoes I wear, they still make my feet hurt. What can I do? Um, see a foot doctor? I thought I'd leave the medical advice to the professionals. I opened the next one. It was written on stiff, cream-colored stationery, and it started off interestingly enough: *Dear Know-It-All, my friend and I like the same girl but I,* and then it must have gotten wet somehow, because the ink ran and for the life of me I couldn't read the rest. Just as well. I'd taken on a similar issue last year. I crumpled it up and tossed it behind me. The last one was in a white envelope with silver trim. I opened it and admired the delicate light green paper it was written on. I loved when people used pretty stationery. It made me feel like they were trying to impress me.

Dear Know-It-All,

The boy I have a crush on says he likes redheads with short hair. I'm a blondish red and my mom won't let me dye my hair redder and I really don't want to cut it short. What do I do?

Sincerely,

Unhappy Blonde

Now, this was something to think about. I lay down on my bed and looked at the ceiling. What if I heard Michael saying something similar, like he was only into girls with short hair. Would I ever cut

it to try and get him to like me? Maybe it wasn't that big an issue. So I cut my hair? It would grow back. But then again, what if I was just cutting it for Michael? That didn't seem right. Also, this boy who says he only likes redheads with short hair sounds so particular. Looks were important, but they weren't the only thing that made someone like someone else. What about personality? He sounded a little shallow to me.

I thought of what Hailey had said about Frank, that his hair was too dark and his ears were too big. What if Frank ever found out that's why Hailey didn't like him? What would he do? What could he do really other than dye his hair! And let's say by magic he could shrink his ears, would Hailey really like him then? I feel like I'd like Michael even if his ears were too big. But the truth was, they weren't and he was painfully adorable, so it was hard to say.

Even though I knew I would have to think about this letter for a while, it felt good to be back in my role as Dear Know-It-All. I folded up the letter and put it under my mattress for safekeeping and

ripped up the others, wrapped them up in tissues, and threw them out. I really needed a shredder. My IM blinked on my computer.

Hey, are u there??

It was Hailey.

I am, I sent back.

Having a homework crisis. 2 much language farts 2 do. Help!!! she wrote.

Poor Hailey. Language arts was her nemesis. It wasn't easy to keep up because of her dyslexia.

Your BFF to the rescue! Checking if my mom can drive me . . .

"Mom," I called. She was in her office, buried in papers as usual. I don't know how my mom did it. Her whole day was full of numbers, since she was a freelance bookkeeper.

"Yes, my dear." She lowered her glasses. "How was school? Did you have a snack?" she asked, knowing that was usually the first thing I did when I walked in the door.

"Hailey's having a homework crisis and needs me to come over ASAP," I said.

"Oh," my mom said, and took off her glasses

immediately. "That sounds serious."

"It's okay if you can't drive me, though," I said, looking down. "I can see you're really, really busy." I was trying to play the sympathy card in case she wasn't in the mood to shuttle me around.

"Sammy," she said, crossing her arms, seeing right through me. "I'm happy to drive you. No need for the drama. You know I just like to plan. But it's your lucky day, because it's quitting time for me," she said, getting up. "Let me just get my keys. I have to run to the store anyway to pick up something for dinner."

My mom is really disciplined. She works from home with no boss watching over her and she gets her work done every day. It's like she spends her day doing homework—math homework no less. I don't know how well I'd do if I were left alone all day every day to do my schoolwork. So I don't think I'm a candidate for homeschooling, but then again, I'd have Mom watching over me.

Allie was in the kitchen making some kind of gross-looking green shake in the blender. She stuffed a bunch of spinach leaves in and turned it on. On the cutting board were the scraps of what looked like zucchini, tomatoes, and celery. She also had her earphones on and plugged into her phone. Allie's phone was her life. If anyone could give a good opinion about texting, it was Allie. I made a mental note to ask her about it later. She had gotten her phone taken away a few times at school for texting.

"Allie!" my mom called over the roaring sound of the blender. Allie had her back to us and was rocking out to her music, oblivious that we were even in the room. "Allie!" my mom called again. I ran up and tapped her on the shoulder, hard. She threw her hands up and screamed and then I screamed because I hadn't expected her to scream.

"What the heck!" Allie said when we stopped screaming. "Are you trying to give me a heart attack?"

"Well, you couldn't hear us! What were we supposed to do? And what in the world are you making?" I said, still yelling over the blender.

She pressed the stop button. "It's a detox green smoothie. Six different kinds of organic veggies are in here," she said, tapping the top of the blender.

"What are you detoxing from?" my mom asked, a worried edge to her voice.

"Just life. Do you know how many toxins we take in at any given moment?"

"It just so happens that I do not, but in the meantime I'm planning to run Sam over Hailey's and stop at the store. You can tell me about the toxins when I get back. Do you want anything special?"

"Remember, I'm vegan now. So no dairy, meat, or eggs. It's great for the earth and great for my skin," she said, and patted her flawless cheeks.

"That's a little too special for me, Allie," Mom said. "I'll make pasta, and you can eat it or make something for yourself."

Allie poured herself a glass of her shake and made a face.

"Disgusting, right?" I said. *Teenager Rethinks Her Vegetable Addiction.*

"No!" she said, still with her I-just-ate-something-disgusting expression on. "It just needs some fruit mixed in."

"Yeah, maybe some fruit and some ice cream. Come on, Mom. Let's go. Hailey's freaking out," I said. Allie was always following some strange trend. One moment she basically lives on pizza, ice cream, and cereal, and the next she's a vegan making spinach shakes. Last month, she went on a gluten-free diet; then it was back to pizza.

She took another swig out of spite but looked like someone had slapped her in the face afterward. Mom and I finally escaped Allie, the detox monster. When I got to Hailey's house, she was in her sweats, pacing back and forth in her kitchen, talking a mile a minute.

"And then I have this essay for a book that I read, but I'm not sure if I really understand it, and then there are those stupid vocab puzzles that make my eyes hurt."

"Really, I think they're fun. Kind of like crosswords," I said.

"Exactly! I *hate* crossword puzzles," Hailey said, throwing her hands up in the air.

"Calm down. It'll be fine," I said.

"Yeah, easy for you to say, Writer Queen of the World."

"Oh, please. Look, you know I can't do half the stuff you're really good at. So at least I have something I'm good at," I said.

After we made a peanut butter and banana sandwich for me and a piece of toast and raspberry jam for her, we got down to business. I helped her organize her essay and we made up funny ways to remember her vocab words.

"Okay, alliteration: the repetition of initial sounds," I said. "Think Hailey Hates Horseradish." I wasn't sure if she did, but if I had to put money on it, I'd say hate.

"OMG." She slapped the counter. "How did you know I hated horseradish?"

"Lucky guess. Does anyone really *like* horseradish?" I asked.

"My dad," Hailey said, crinkling up her face. "He puts it on his sandwiches."

"You should have seen what Allie was cooking up in the kitchen today. She's decided she's vegan now and made a smoothie thing out of spinach.

You would have loved it," I said, taking a big bite of my sandwich.

"Sounds like I might have if she had just added horseradish," Hailey said, and I cracked up.

"Okay, okay. Next. Hyperbole: an extreme exaggeration. Frank's ears are as big as flying saucers."

"Hey, that's mean," she said, and actually looked hurt. Hmmm, I wondered if a crush was developing.

"Well, it's a hyperbole, an extreme exaggeration, not the truth! And that's what you think, not me."

"Well, I never said they were *that* big," Hailey responded, still sounding a little irked.

I decided to leave it alone and just nod. I didn't want to make her upset, and it would be totally cool if she liked Frank. We did some more vocab words, and I helped her do an outline for her essay. She was in much better shape.

"Thanks, O Homework Genie," she said, throwing her arms around me.

"That's what friends are for," I said, and

returned the hug. "Now you can help me do a handstand!"

"Really?" she said, jumping off her seat with excitement.

"No, not really. Unless you want to see my peanut butter and banana sandwich again."

"Ewww," she said. Her phone made a *ding*. She looked at it.

"Who is it?" I said.

"My dad," Hailey said. "Ever since he's gotten the hang of texting, he texts the entire family every day—what the weather's like out, since he's first to leave the house, what he's having for lunch, and what train he's going to be on so we know what time he's getting home. It's kind of cute and kind of annoying."

"That sounds kind of cute and kind of annoying," I said. "My mom never texts us. Do you ever text during class?" I asked, thinking about my article.

"*Moi?*" Hailey said, batting her eyes, pretending to be innocent. "Never!"

"No, really," I said in a low, serious tone.

She nibbled at her toast. "Maybe once, but honestly, I don't really text that much. I IM lots when I'm home, and as you know, I'm always on Buddybook, but usually when I'm at school I actually like to talk to people in person. What a concept! Now, my dad is different story."

I laughed. "Well, Mr. Trigg wants me and Michael to do an article on texting."

"Like in what way? That people text. Doesn't sound like breaking news."

"Well, I guess we can write about how rampant it is and how people feel about the new detention rule. But you're right, it's not that exciting to me either."

"I'm sure you guys will find something interesting about it that will get everyone talking. You always do."

"Thanks, Hails, but that remains to be seen." I slumped down in my seat, holding up my head with my hands. I hoped Michael would come up with a more interesting spin, because I was stumped.

Chapter 4

ONE DOWN, SEVERAL MORE TO GO

★ ★ ★

"We have to do a poll," Michael said as he came rushing up to me, Hailey, and Kate at lunch the next day. We stopped our conversation and stared at him.

"Hi. How are you, Michael? Have a seat." Hailey gestured to a chair.

"Sorry," Michael said, smiling sheepishly. "I'm just a little keyed up."

"Wait, what do you mean?" I asked, unwrapping a granola bar. Hailey picked at yet another plate of rice, which she ate every day for lunch. Maybe Allie needed to give Hailey one of her spinach smoothies; then Hailey might appreciate other foods more. Kate was delicately eating a turkey sandwich, but then again, she could be eating a rack of ribs and she would eat them delicately.

Michael pulled out his chair and sat down. He did look a little keyed up. His blue eyes were wide. His hair was a little messy, which of course on him looked totally cute.

"Frank got detention for texting," Michael said, a little breathlessly. "He was just texting his mom in the hallway to tell her what time he'd be home after practice!"

One Down, Several More to Go. This was just the beginning, I thought.

"The school has gone mad!" Kate exclaimed.

"Wow, poor Frank," Hailey said, looking very concerned. Was I crazy, or was this more evidence of the fact that Hailey was crushing on Frank even though she wouldn't admit it?

"That's awful," I said. "This new rule is really ridiculous. People text now to communicate. It has to be worked into our lives at school without distracting people in class. There's got to be a way."

"That's why I think we have to set up a poll online. That way we'll know what the majority thinks. We could do it through the *Voice* site. It would get people interested in the article before it even came out. More points for technology."

"That's a great idea," I said. Just then Frank came over. He looked really down.

"Frank," Hailey said. "Michael told us about your detention. That sounds so unfair." Then she did her little hair flip, which she only did when she was flirting.

"Thanks," he said, looking at her. "It's okay. But my mom is furious with the school that I got in trouble for texting her important information. If I had called her on the office phone, which would have taken more time, I wouldn't have gotten in trouble."

"If this rule makes no sense, why do you think they did it?" Kate asked.

"I think it's because texting is an unconscious habit the school is trying to break," I theorized. "For most kids, it's obvious that it's not okay to text during class, but I see kids do it all the time, probably because they're just so used to texting all the time, they don't even think about it."

"Well," said Hailey, pointing her fork at Frank. "This will certainly make people think twice.

Maybe we need an extreme rule like this to snap us out of it."

"Glad I could be of service," Frank said bitterly.

"No," Hailey said, looking worried. "I meant the rule, not what happened to you."

"I gotta go," Frank said. "Catch y'all later."

"Hey, Frankie," called Michael. "I'll walk out with you. Sam, I'll text you, um"—he cleared his throat—"tonight about putting up the poll."

"Sounds good," I answered. Then we watched in silence as he and Frank left the cafeteria.

"Was I obnoxious?" Hailey wailed. "I hadn't meant to be at all."

"No, you weren't. I think Frank's just bummed that he was made an example of. I would be too, but then again, he knew the rule."

"How can you be taking the school's side?" Hailey asked, now even more upset.

"I'm not," I replied.

"I think what Sam means is that—," Kate said, trying to step in and lower the tension.

"I need some air," Hailey said, getting up.

"Are you mad at me now?" I asked.

Hailey took a deep breath. "No, no. I just feel a little stupid. Listen, I'll meet you after school and we can walk home together."

My shoulders relaxed. "Okay," I said in a small voice.

"I think I'm going to take off too," Kate said.

"Sure, go right ahead," I said. What was with everyone today?

After school, Hailey and I walked home together, but we were both pretty quiet, lost in our own thoughts. It was still warm out, and I started longing for the ease of summer again. Suddenly school seemed so complicated. The texting article now just made me feel angry at the school because of what happened to Frank. At the same time, I could understand that the administrators might need to take a stand. I had done a little research, and it was true what Jessica said about the *New York Times* article—teenagers send and receive texts eighty times a day. I didn't, but I was still pretty new to having my own phone and I also wasn't one of those people who are addicted to their phone. Allie was, though. I wondered what her number would be. Maybe the poll would clarify things a little more.

"You sure you're not mad?" I asked Hailey as we were about to go our separate ways to our houses.

"Promise. I just felt bad that I made Frank feel worse."

"Hailey, are you sure you don't have a crush on him?" I asked, staring her dead in the eye.

"Sorry, O Matchmaker, but he's just a friend to me," Hailey said lightly. "Later, alligator!"

I couldn't help but think about poor Frank's ears again. If only they were a little smaller, he'd be in luck.

When I got home, Allie was in the kitchen again. I could hear the blender. Good grief!

This time the contents looked purple instead of green, and there were blueberries and strawberry tops scattered around the countertop. A promising sign.

"What are you making now?" I asked, sitting on the bar stool at the kitchen counter. "Is Mom home?"

"No, she'll be back in an hour," Allie replied absentmindedly.

"Good, now I don't have to get up and put this away," I said, letting my bag drop to the floor. There was nothing my mom hated more than stepping over our school bags.

"It's called my superdelicious berryrific soy smoothie!" Allie announced. "I'll give you some. You could use some antioxidants."

"You didn't tell me what's in it."

"Blueberries, raspberries, strawberries, and soy milk," she said, pouring me a big glass of it.

I took it and looked inside. It was purple and frothy. It smelled pretty good. I took a sip. It was creamy, sweet, and tangy.

"Not bad," I said, and took another sip.

"And you can't even taste the kale, can you?" she asked, a mischievous sparkle in her eye.

"Kale! You said berries!" I exclaimed.

"So you'd taste it. Berries and kale."

I looked inside again. It did actually taste yummy. Not a bad way to eat kale. I shrugged and sipped away. Maybe it would make my skin look better. ***Magical Smoothie Clears Up Skin Instantly!*** Hey, you never know. Lately I was getting some bumps on my chin, which I was not happy about. Gosh, what if I really started breaking out? That would ruin all chances of getting Michael to see me as more than a friend, or would it? That made me think of my Dear Know-It-All letter.

"Allie," I said as she leaned against the counter sipping her own serving of smoothie. "Would you ever change your appearance for a boy?"

"Like, in what way?" she asked, and squinted at me. Now I had her full attention. She probably liked giving advice more than I did, but I was the one-and-only Dear Know-It-All. I couldn't wait for that day in the future when I'd finally be able to tell Allie how I secretly wrote Dear Know-It-All for two years. I'd make sure to bring a camera and record the expression on her face. "Like, if the boy you really liked only liked girls with short hair or something. Would you cut your hair for him?"

"No way! Are you kidding me?"

"Just asking," I said. I actually hadn't expected Allie to have such a strong reaction to the question. She lived for attention from boys, but then again she had a new boyfriend basically every three months, so she didn't have to try so hard. "Well, boys always seem to like you. Maybe you don't have to think about things like this."

"You have a smoothie mustache," Allie said, and pointed at me.

I swiped the back of my hand over my mouth.

"Still, my answer remains the same," Allie went on. "And not every boy I've liked has liked me back, believe it or not."

"Really?" I said.

"Really."

Well, that at least made me feel better. It wasn't easy having a blond boy magnet for a sister. I was even suspicious that Michael had a crush on her. At least Allie would never reciprocate. He was too young for her, and she knew I'd never speak to her again. Allie was a lot of things, but she was also loyal. Michael had a couple of pretty cute brothers, though, and she was friends with them.

I wouldn't even like her dating one of them. Too close for comfort.

"Okay, I think I've had my fill of antioxidants," I said, putting the half-finished smoothie down. I went into my room and poked around at CNN.com and Huffington Post. My phone beeped and I grabbed it.

`Let's put up the poll 2nite,` said a text from Michael.

`K. How about this question: Do you break the texting rule at school?` I responded.

`Perfect! I'll get it going!` he wrote back.

`Thanks!`

We were a perfect pair in that respect. I was faster with content and he was faster with the tech stuff. I decided to do a Google search to get more facts about teen texting. Lots of stuff came up, but one thing that caught my eye was an article about the Centers for Disease Control. They had just done a study and found that one-third of teens admit to texting while driving. I guess any habit that leads to a lot of distraction can be dangerous. Sneaking a text here and there at school was probably harmless, but it could lead to stuff that might be really bad. It added another complicated layer to a subject that suddenly didn't seem so boring anymore.

Allie knocked on my door and then came in without waiting for my answer.

"You always make me knock," I said, whipping around in my chair.

"I knocked," she said.

"Yeah, but I didn't say anything," I said, turning back to the screen.

"It's urgent. I was thinking about your question." She flung herself on my bed and propped up her head in her hands.

"Yeah?" I spun around on my desk chair to face her.

"I changed my mind. It's only hair. It will grow back. Why not try a new look?"

"Really? So you would cut your hair for a guy?" I asked, wondering what had changed her mind.

"Well, no, I wouldn't do it just for the guy. If I found a cute haircut that I wanted to try, I might take a risk, but I'd never do it if I didn't want to do it. You can't lose yourself in the hope that someone would like you better if you just looked different," she said, and went over to my mirror. She piled her hair on top of her head and checked her look from different angles. Then she let her hair tumble down. "If he doesn't like me the way I am, that's it for him." She sat down on the edge of my bed and smiled. "Boys are like trains. If you miss one, there's always another one in five minutes."

"Maybe for you," I said, and crossed my arms over my chest.

Allie narrowed her eyes suspiciously. "Did Michael Lawrence tell you to cut your hair? Don't you dare! It's your best feature."

I wasn't sure if that was a compliment. "Michael Lawrence has nothing to do with it. I swear."

"Good," she said. She hopped up. "Let's see." She came over and pulled my hair up and glanced at me from both sides. "Yeah, keep it long."

"I plan to," I said. "Now I have top-secret work to do."

"Yeah, right," Allie said as she headed out the door. Little did she know.

Chapter 5

GIRL GETS ARRESTED FOR TEXTING IN SCHOOL

★ ★ ★

The next morning I checked out the poll results. Michael had put it up the night before, and immediately people started responding to it. It was on the *Voice* site, and Mr. Trigg got permission for us to send out a blast e-mail to the whole school so people would know it was there. People had the choice to respond to it anonymously or give their names, but everyone seemed to go with the anonymous choice, probably to make sure they didn't get in trouble. Mr. Trigg had said it would be helpful for the administration to see it, so they could be more in touch with the student community. I'd heard about three more people getting detention for texting in the last couple of days. People were not happy.

The poll program automatically totaled the percentages of yeses and no's. More than forty percent of people admitted they snuck texts during the day. That was even more than I'd thought. I texted Michael on my way to school.

Great job on the poll! Crazy response!

After I sent it, I checked my phone just before I walked in the doors to see if he had gotten back to me. Nothing. I sat through my language arts, earthonomics, and science classes, and still hadn't seen Michael yet. I was dying to check my phone, which was tucked away in my locker. At lunch I sat with Hailey, Kate, and Jenna.

"So, question of the day," I said to everyone, getting out my notebook, wanting to get some quotes for the article. "Do you guys text in school, even with the new rule?"

"Really, who doesn't? I still never did or would in class, but it's not hard to send a few messages between classes," said Jenna. "I don't really think the school has a right to stop us from doing that.

And I always tell my mom what time I'm going to be home. I still do it, and she hasn't told me not to."

"How have you not gotten caught?" I asked. Since the rule, I haden't touched my phone at school.

"You just pretend you're getting something out of your backpack," she said. Everyone nodded knowingly.

"Really," said Jenna. "I don't know how you just stop texting. It's crazy."

I guess it was kind of an addiction. The more you texted, the more you needed to text.

I still hadn't seen Michael. After lunch I couldn't stand it anymore. Maybe Michael was sick today? I probably wouldn't have even cared that much, but because I'd sent him a text, now suddenly it was like this major itch I couldn't scratch. I guess this is how other people felt all day long.

I went to my locker to get a book out. I looked at my bag. How big a deal would it be if I looked at my phone? I opened my bag, like Jenna said, and pretended I was getting something out of it.

I poked my head out of my locker to see if any teachers, or worse, the principal, was walking by. It looked clear. I felt around in my bag and turned over my phone so I could see the screen. Just as I was squinting to see if I had any messages, a hand was on my shoulder.

"Ms. Martone, you'll have to come with me," the voice said in this weird deep tone. I froze and dropped my phone into my bag. I couldn't believe it. I wasn't even texting, technically, just looking. Was I really going to get in trouble for that? *Girl Gets Arrested for Texting in School.* At least that's what it felt like would happen. My mom was not going to be happy.

I turned around, and grinning back at me was Michael Lawrence.

"That was *so* not funny!" I yelled at him.

"Easy, Pasty. I just couldn't resist," Michael said. He even had the nerve to use his stupid nickname for me.

"Well, it's your fault. You should have texted me back right away," I said.

"I didn't even see your text until lunch. You

know I'm not much of a texter."

"Well then, how did you see it at lunch? You weren't at lunch anyway." I smoothed my hair, still collecting myself.

"Well, I wasn't at lunch because I went to the library to cram for a science quiz. And sometimes I sneak looks in my locker too. Who doesn't? But thanks for the text. The poll might just have an effect on the new rule. This article's starting to have potential," he said.

"I know. I got a couple of good quotes." Something was a little different about Michael today. He looked a little extra awesome, but I couldn't figure out why.

"I cut my hair. I know it's really short," he said.

I just looked at him, not sure what to say. Had he read my mind?

"That's why you were looking at me strangely, right?" he said, running his fingers through his dark, spiky hair. "Is it really lame?"

"No, not at all. I was actually thinking that it looks good," I said.

"You're lying just to make me feel better," he said.

"Not at all. You look very stylish." I was really touched that he actually cared what I thought. If only he knew how truthful I was being.

"Would you ever cut your hair for a girl?" I asked, hoping he wouldn't say he had or something like that, because I would know the girl he'd cut his hair for was not me.

He laughed. "I don't think so. Why?"

"Allie said she'd cut her hair for a boy she likes," I blurted out. Why was I even telling him this?

Michael considered this for a minute. "Allie would look nice with short hair. She's got a really pretty face. She could carry it off," he said thoughtfully.

Wait, what? How had I even gotten myself in this conversation? *Middle School Student Wishes for Vanishing Powers.* The thought of Michael picturing Allie with short hair, or picturing her in any way at all, turned my stomach. Did he think she was prettier than I was?

"Um, yeah. Well, gotta run," I said.

Michael seemed a little confused. "Okay, but

hold on. We need to get together to go over our notes for the article."

"Text me," I called over my shoulder as I hurried away, feeling a little light-headed. All I could think of was Michael thinking of Allie with some cute pixie cut.

The moment I got home, I called Hailey. I needed a live voice to talk to. This was not something an encouraging text could solve. Luckily, Allie wasn't home and Mom was still working in her office. I took the phone into the kitchen.

"Michael is in love with Allie," I wailed when I heard Hailey's voice.

"Back up a minute. What are you talking about?" Hailey said.

"I told Michael that Allie said she'd cut her hair for a boy, which she didn't really say, but she sort of did. For some reason, I made it seem like that to Michael, and then he said that she would look really great with short hair, like prettier than me, or something like that. Allie said boys are like trains, but I don't want Michael to be a train like, boom he's there and then he's gone. So I freaked out for the rest of the day, and now I'm calling you." I let it out all in one breath. In fact, I was out of breath. I needed to calm down.

"Have you lost your mind?" Hailey said. "Trains? Boys are like trains?"

"Yeah, that's what Allie said. As in, if you miss one, there's always another one in five minutes," I said. I needed a snack. Maybe a bowl of cheese popcorn would help me relax.

"Hmmm. She has a point," Hailey said, considering it.

"Hailey? Really?"

"Well, they can be like that. I've had a few crushes come and go, and I know there will always be another boy. Friends are what matter the most."

I agreed, but the problem was, or maybe it wasn't a problem, but what made things complicated with Michael is that he was a good friend of mine and my crush all bundled into one.

"Yeah, but," I said, about to explain it to Hailey.

"I know. I know. Michael's not like other boys."

"I don't know. Maybe he is. He's probably just

friends with me so that once in a while he gets to come to my house and gawk at my sister."

Hailey started laughing so hard on the other end of the line that she began to choke a little bit.

"Are you okay?" I asked, half-concerned, half-annoyed. I didn't think what I'd said was funny at all. I held the phone to my ear, opened the bag of cheddar popcorn, and poured myself a big bowl.

She coughed and laughed a little more, then cleared her throat.

"I'm, ah, fine. I got a little"—she coughed one more time—"carried away. That train thing just . . . Okay, sorry. Listen, I'm just going to tell you this once. Snap. Out. Of. It. You're awesome and beautiful, and Michael loves you even though he can't admit it, or is afraid it will ruin your friendship or something. But you're not just some cute girl to him. You're more than that—short hair, long hair, whatever. And for the record, I think you'd look awesome with short hair."

I sat on the bar stool, swinging my legs, and chewed my popcorn. How had I let my thoughts get so out of control? Michael was my friend, a real friend, not just a subway kind of boy. Allie was pretty. Of course he would notice that, and I was the one who'd brought up the whole ridiculous question. It didn't mean he thought she was prettier than me.

"Sam, you still there?" Hailey asked in a small, worried voice.

"Yeah, I'm here." I sighed. "Thanks for saying that."

"Why did you tell him all that anyway?" she asked.

"I have no idea," I said, and stuffed another handful of popcorn in my face.

After I got off the phone, I went into my room and stared in the mirror. I had nice green eyes. My hair was definitely shinier than Allie's. I had a little blemish on my chin, but nothing a little cover-up couldn't take care of. I got a few hair clips and started to pin up sections of my hair to see what I'd look like with it short. Then I put a little lip gloss on and took a picture with my phone. I stared at it for a while. It just didn't look like me. I took a few more angles. Cute, but still it was like I was looking at someone else. I put my phone away and started on my homework.

"How was your day?" Mom asked me at dinner.

I took a bite of pork chop.

"Pretty good," I said. Where would I begin? "I am thinking about getting my hair cut."

Allie glared at me over her mashed potatoes and broccoli. She'd added some fake tofu meat to it instead of pork chops and had forced my mom to make the mashed potatoes without milk. They were fine, just not as creamy. I was getting tired of Allie's fads dominating the whole house. I squirmed in my chair a little.

"What do you mean?" Allie said. "I thought we agreed that you weren't going to do that, rememberrrrr?" she said in a weird singsongy voice.

"I just think I might look cool, like, for me." Here I was again in a conversation I started that I suddenly wanted no part of. What was wrong with me?

My mom was looking back and forth at Allie and me. "Well, who else would it be for?" she asked.

"A boy," Allie said.

"No, not a boy," I barked back at Allie. "I just think Hailey's hair is so cute short and maybe it would look good on me. What's the big deal?"

"Okay," my mom said. "I get the feeling there's some background to this that I don't know about. Want to clue me in?"

"No!" Allie and I both said at the same time. I crossed my arms and we were silent for a bit.

"Well," Mom said. "Lovely having dinner with you both."

Allie finally started talking about the auditions for her dance concert, and I just sat quietly, not wanting to open my mouth again today.

Later that night, when I was trying to fall asleep, I kept grabbing my phone off my night table and staring at my short hair picture again. It kind of looked cute, but I knew it wasn't me. I just kept hearing Michael saying the same words over and over again. *Allie's got a really pretty face. She could carry it off.* It echoed in my head like I was possessed. Did he think my face was pretty enough to carry it off? Maybe I should just cut my hair to prove that I could. I put the phone away and tried to sleep again, but sleep wasn't not finding me.

I got out of bed, stared at my photo for another minute, and then turned on the computer. Maybe the only way I could get this stuff off my mind was reply to Unhappy Blonde.

Dear Unhappy Blonde,

There are lots of things we sometimes wish we could change about ourselves. Maybe we wish we were a better student, or a better dresser, or were taller or shorter. Some of these things we can change and some we can't . I guess you could change your hair for this guy, but what if the next day you hear him talking about only liking girls with green eyes and yours are brown? Or he decides he likes blondes after all. You shouldn't change your appearance just because a guy wants you to. You should make changes for yourself, because you are the one who s going to have to live with it, guy or no guy. He should appreciate you just the way you are. In my opinion, if he asks you to cut your hair, he doesn't make the cut.

There! That's how I really felt about things. I hoped I wouldn't give myself away since I had already talked about cutting hair for a guy with both Allie and Michael, but I had a plan of what to say when they asked me. I would tell them I overheard someone else talking about this very issue, which was why I'd started thinking about it. I would wonder out loud if that person was either Dear Know-It-All or Unhappy Blonde and send them on a dead-end hunt.

I stood in front of my mirror and brushed my hair until it was shiny as silk. When I lay back down, I finally drifted off to sleep.

Chapter 6

ICE CREAM SOLVES WORLD'S PROBLEMS

★ ★ ★

"So, are you finally over it?" Hailey asked as we walked into Scoops, our favorite ice-cream place in town. We were meeting for a little treat after school. I certainly could use it.

"Over it?" I shrugged. I needed to order before I talked about anything. "A double scoop of Crazy Cookie and Double-Trouble Chocolate in a waffle cone, please, with rainbow sprinkles," I said to the girl behind the counter.

"Wow, impressive," Hailey said to me. "That sounds amazing. I'll have the same," she said to the counter girl.

We got our cones and sat down at one of the tables. I took a big bite, a little bit of Crazy Cookie, a little bit of Double-Trouble Chocolate, and the edge of the waffle cone, all together in one sweet chocolaty creamy crunchy combination. Heaven. *Ice Cream Solves World's Problems.* Or at least mine, for just a few minutes. Now I was ready to talk.

"I think I'm over it. Let's not even talk about it anymore," I said, taking another bite.

"Okay," Hailey replied, looking a little disappointed.

"Tell me something interesting about you. Are you sure you don't like Frank? Is it just because of his ears and his dark hair?"

Hailey rolled her eyes at me. "Will you leave it alone? Why do you want me to have a crush on him so bad?"

"Oh, I don't know. Maybe I'm just bored and trying to stir something up."

"Well, stir up something else," Hailey said. "Trust me. You'll be the first to know when someone catches my eye. Right now I'm just focusing on soccer, schoolwork, and having fun with you!"

"Sounds like a plan," I said. I wasn't really bored, but I was tired. We were just finishing up our ice cream when Jeff, the *Voice* photographer, came in. He ordered a dish of what looked like

Mint-Chip Madness. I waved at him, and he came and sat down with us.

"You know, I'm trying to get some more 'around town' kind of candids. Can I take a few pictures of you guys?" he asked.

Hailey and I looked at each other. Hailey touched her hair. I wiped my mouth just to make sure there wasn't a big blob of Double-Trouble Chocolate on my chin.

"I guess so," I said, still looking at Hailey doubtfully.

"Yes!" she said, and flung her arm around me. "Normally, I have very strict policies for the paparazzi, but I'll allow this one exception."

We mugged for the camera, gave our best famous movie-star looks, and by the time Jeff was finished taking photos, we were practically on the floor, hysterical laughing.

"Wow. I think I got some great ones," Jeff said, flipping through the pics on his digital camera. "You guys are good subjects."

"Yes, yes." I waved my hand dramatically at him. "Just make sure you send them to my agent."

"Right," said Jeff. "Well I'll let you two get back to your ice cream."

Just then my phone *ding*ed. I looked down to see the text.

When are we going to meet???

"It's Michael," I said to Hailey.

"Ooh, what does he want?"

"I think he wants to meet for our texting article," I told her, still looking at my phone.

"Well, I say no better time than the present!" She banged the table with her fist.

I jumped. "Sheesh! You mean here?" I asked, looking around. There were only three tables.

"Probably not, unless you're going to get another waffle cone. Maybe the coffee shop next door?"

"But we're hanging out," I said, even though I thought it would be great to meet Michael now. I didn't have a lot of homework tonight, so it would be great to get some more things hammered out and to start writing. I felt a little behind on the article, and even though I'd gotten some decent quotes and the poll info, we still needed more opinions from both the students and the faculty. I didn't want to ditch Hailey, though.

"I have a big test on Monday and my mom's going to help me study, so I should go anyway."

"Are you sure?" I asked. "I can meet him another time."

Hailey nodded. "Really," she said. "Meet him now."

"You're the boss," I said.

"I am?" Hailey said, fluffing her hair. "Well, that's good news, because I always want to be the boss."

"Don't I know it," I said as I texted Michael back.

Hailey put her hands on her hips. "Hey!" she said.

How about the Java Stop in five minutes? I typed, naming the coffee place next door. "You know, whenever I text someone," I said to Hailey, "I stress out until I hear from them. Like, as soon as I hit the send button, I start to feel all anxious. Does that ever happen to you?" I asked.

"I guess so. I certainly would if I were texting my Michael Lawrence, if I, like, you know, had one."

"You make it sound like something you pick up at the grocery store. Michael Lawrences on sale this week. Two for one."

"Ha-ha. The store would probably sell out."

"Well, that's nice to say . . . I think." I imagined trying to explain the compliment to Michael. I didn't think it would translate well. My phone *ding*ed again. I looked down.

Great! I can b there in ten, he responded.

Then I let out a breath. "Okay, hold the phone," I said, putting my hand up in a "stop" position. "In ten minutes, I'm going to be hanging out in the Java Stop with Michael Lawrence," I said, the truth of it just dawning on me. "Do I look okay?" I asked, smoothing my hair and pinching my cheeks, like Allie had taught me. I don't think Michael and I had ever been there together. We had only been "in public" alone maybe two or three times.

"You look fab, except for that chocolate ice cream all over your face."

"What?" I cried, wiping frantically at my chin and mouth.

"Just kidding," Hailey said as she stood up and grabbed her backpack.

I walked out with her, said good-bye, and then went into the Java Stop. I stood at the counter looking at the chalk-drawn menu. I wasn't in the mood for anything sugary after my ice cream, so I ordered an unsweetened iced tea. I found a table in the back. I sipped my tea and waited. Luckily, no one I knew was there, except for a few high school kids I vaguely recognized. Not that I didn't want anyone to see me and Michael. It just made me more nervous to feel like we were being watched by people we knew.

Michael came in and didn't see me at first. He ordered something at the counter and then turned around, glancing this way and that, and still didn't see me. I waved, but he just turned around and sat down at a table near the front, which was probably what I should have done in the first place. A few tables full of kids were almost blocking my way, but I could still see him sipping his drink and checking his phone. It was kind of fun to spy on him like this. I waited a few more moments and then decided to text him instead of getting up and going over to him, to get us in the mind-set of our article.

Look past the table in front of you and to the left.

I saw him see the text and look up, almost alarmed. I gave him a big smile and a wave, and he saw me and smiled back. Then he picked up his cup and came over.

"You're full of surprises today, Paste," he said, sitting down.

"And why's that?" I asked, searching in my bag for my notebook.

"Oh, I don't know. I'm just sensing a new spontaneity in you. I like it," he said.

I looked down to hide the redness creeping into my cheeks. Spontaneity? Would Michael like me more if I were more spontaneous? I always thought he liked that I was pretty organized and planned out about things. I did love my lists.

"You call this spontaneous?" I said, showing him my list/outline for the article, neatly written out in numbered and lettered sections.

"Well, no. But something's a little different about you this year," he said knowingly. Honestly, I didn't really know what he was talking about. Maybe he just wished I was different and was trying to make me that way. Was that a crazy thing to think? I turned to a blank page in my notebook.

"These are my . . . spontaneous . . . thoughts on our article. Ready?" I said.

"Ready as I'll ever be, Pasty. Actually, I might need to come up with a new nickname for you."

"While you think about that incredibly important thing, I'm going to continue my thought," I said, pointing my pencil at him.

"Okay, sorry," he said, smiling sheepishly and sinking down in his chair a little bit.

"We just don't have a hook here. I mean, fine, we text too much in school and now the school makes a rule that we can't and we're all upset about it. That's it? We need something more than that."

"I agree. Hit me with your spontaneity, Pasty. I mean Fancy-Free!" His eyes sparkled.

"Are you serious? Fancy-Free? I don't think so.

But how's this for spontaneous? We need a bigger story here, something we can follow. Something that will add a little more drama to the situation," I said, tapping my pencil on my notebook. I took a sip of my tea.

"Yeah, I'm listening," Michael said, and leaned back in his chair, putting his hands behind his head.

"How about . . . we . . . um." I still wasn't sure what I wanted to say. I thought about the poll and how it was cool to get people's honest behavior and feedback. What if we dug a little deeper into people's real experiences with texting? A brainstorm was forming. I stuck my pencil in the air. "How about we invite people to participate in an experiment!"

"What kind of experiment?" Michael asked, now leaning forward in his chair.

"Where we ask people not to text for twenty-four hours," I announced.

"I like it." He thought for a moment. "And then we can ask them to e-mail us their experiences," he continued.

"Yes! Maybe we could get some teachers to participate too. They may be just as addicted to texting as the students are outside of class. It levels the playing field. We all have to deal with the good parts and bad parts about technology. It's not just the kids who are dealing with it."

"I love it! I'll clear it with Mr. Trigg to send out another blast *Voice* e-mail. Hopefully, we can get it out tonight. Nice one, Fancy-Free," he said, and held up his hand for a high-five. I reached over the table to give him one and knocked over my drink. Luckily it spilled to the side, not in Michael's lap.

"Oh no," I exclaimed, grabbing a bunch of napkins from the container on the table. Michael grabbed some and helped me. We both wiped the table up as fast as we could. Then we knelt on the floor, since a big puddle had formed to the side of the table. I really wasn't paying attention to anything else but trying to clean it up as fast as I could when, *bam*, our heads crashed right into each other.

"Ow!" I said, holding my forehead.

"Are you okay?" Michael said, looking up at

me. Our faces were an inch away from each other. The whole scenario was making me dizzy. I got up quickly, still rubbing my head.

"Oh, I'm fine," I said, as if I didn't have a huge throbbing pain in the center of my head. "Are you?" I asked. His forehead looked okay. He wasn't rubbing it or anything.

"I think you got the worst of it. I guess my head is harder than yours." He smiled.

"I think it might be," I said, still rubbing the sore spot.

Michael looked at me with his mouth open. "Gee, thanks," he said.

"You're the one who brought it up!" I nudged him in the arm.

"Wait here," he said. He went up to the counter and talked to the barista. A minute later, he came back holding a small plastic bag of ice and a new iced tea for me.

"Here you go," he said. "Now, sit down and take a moment to ice the bump. It will keep the swelling down."

"Aww, Mickey, you're a class act," I said,

holding the ice to my forehead.

"Thanks. So are you. Just try to be a little less, uh, spontaneous next time . . . Spilly."

Well, I certainly deserved that one.

Chapter 7

RUMOR SPREADS THAT CLUMSY KISS CAUSES INJURY

★ ★ ★

"How did you get that bump?" my mother asked when I got home. I ran and looked in the bathroom mirror. There was a raised red circle the size of a quarter on the right side of my forehead. Ugh. Michael Lawrence did have a hard head. I came back out.

"It's a long story," I said, collapsing in a kitchen bar stool.

My mom got an ice pack out of the freezer and sat down next to me. She gently put it on my forehead. Michael's ice pack had long since melted.

"I've got all the time in the world," Mom responded, adjusting the position of the ice pack. Then I heard the front door open. Oh brother. I didn't want to explain this in front of Allie.

"What happened?" she exclaimed when she came into the kitchen and gave me a once-over, throwing her bag on a stool.

I sighed. "Nothing."

"Did you walk into a wall again?" Allie asked, going to the pantry. She took out a bag of potato chips and started munching away. My mom and I both looked at her.

"These are vegan, you know!" she barked at us over a mouthful.

"So, Sammy, what happened?" Mom said, turning her focus on me again. "That's a pretty mean bump."

"Okay, fine. I bumped heads with Michael Lawrence."

Allie almost spit out her potato chips, she started laughing so hard. Even my mom was trying to hold back her smile, but she wasn't doing a very good job of it.

"Did you guys try to kiss and miss?" Allie said when she collected herself.

Perfect. I could just see Allie telling her friends that. *Rumor Spreads that Clumsy*

Kiss Causes Injury. "No!" I said, getting off the kitchen stool. "Forget it." I took the ice pack and stomped off to my room. Not only did I have a huge bump on my head, but now I had to be ridiculed by my family. But the truth was, it had all been worth it. Michael was so sweet to me the rest of our time at the Java Stop. There was something romantic about it all, him taking care of me like that, with the ice pack and the iced tea. He even kept asking me to take off the ice pack so he could check the bump. They could laugh if they wanted to. It was kind of special. Although I would have preferred a less hazardous moment to get him to pay so much attention to me.

There was a knock on my door.

"Yeah?" I called.

"It's me, honey," Mom said.

"Come in," I replied, and lay back on my bed, still holding the ice pack on my head, and closed my eyes.

"Let me check it." My mom sat on the edge of the bed. "It's gone down a lot. You can barely see it anymore."

"Really?" I asked, and sat up quickly. "Ow." It still kind of hurt when I moved fast.

"Take it easy." She pushed me gently on the shoulder so I'd lie down again. "Sorry we laughed, Sammy. Or to be accurate, Allie laughed and I smiled," she said, and smiled again. "But I really do want to know exactly how you bumped heads. I assume it wasn't the reason Allie said."

I took a deep breath. "Oh, for crying out loud, Mom. I spilled my tea at the Java Stop, and we both got on the floor to clean it up and then we kind of crashed into each other."

"Oh. Gee, what does the other guy look like?"

"What are you talking about?" I said. Sometimes my mom used sayings that totally confused me.

"You know, the other guy in the fight?" she said.

"There wasn't any fight," I said, now getting frustrated again.

"Sammy, where'd your sense of humor go? I'm just kidding. I was just wondering if Michael has a bump on his head too."

"No. I think he has a harder head than I do," I said in all seriousness.

My mom started to grin. I laughed. I couldn't help it. "Yeah, yeah, I know it's kind of funny."

"So how's the paper going? Are you on target to hit your deadline?"

"Yeah, pretty much. I finished the Dear Know-It-All letter, and the texting article is shaping up. We're going to ask kids if they want to try not texting for twenty-four hours and report back their experiences."

"That's interesting. Well, I'm sure if you and Michael put your heads together, it'll be great," she said, and broke out into another big smile.

"Mom!" I said, and shoved her shoulder lightly. "You're worse than Allie."

"Sorry. Couldn't help myself," Mom said, still grinning. "In all seriousness, though, it sounds like a really good idea. Very timely."

"Want to join in the experiment?" I asked her.

"Oh, sweetie, I wish I could, but I mostly text my clients, and they're expecting me to get back to them quickly. I can't go missing in action."

I understood that. It's not like she was texting her friends all day, which is mostly what kids did. She actually used it for her work. Sometimes I worried that when I grew up, nobody would actually want to talk to each other anymore. Maybe this article would make people think about why they liked to text so much.

After Mom left, I messaged Hailey on my computer.

I crashed heads with Michael at the Java Stop.

In a few minutes, she wrote back.

Oh no! Like you got in a big argument?

No, I mean like I spilled my tea and when we were cleaning it up—bang! I texted back.

I M laughing really hard now, she wrote.

Thanks for your concern, I wrote back. Why did everyone think this was so hilarious? Didn't anyone actually care about my head?

Oh, and (ha-ha) are you ok (he-he)? she replied.

It was actually kind of romantic. He got me an ice pack.

Awwww. Glad ur ok.

I'll survive, I wrote. Sigh.

Monday morning, I sat up in bed and felt my forehead. My head didn't hurt anymore and I didn't feel a bump, which was a good sign. I looked in the mirror. The bump was gone. It was just a little red in the spot, but nothing really noticeable. I still had a little pimple on my chin that I wasn't thrilled about. Oh, well, at least I didn't have a huge bruise on my forehead that people would ask me about. That would be fun to explain at school.

I was walking down the hall to my first class when I felt a tap on my shoulder. I looked one way, but no one was there. Then I felt a tap on my other shoulder.

"Okay, stop it, please," I said, looking in that direction.

"You seem to be back to a hundred percent, Spilly," Michael said from my other side. Then he peered at my face. I hoped he wasn't staring at my pimple.

"No sign of injury," he said. "Good. I was worried you'd come in with a big old lump on your head and I'd have to feel worse than I already do."

"No worries. I'm as good as new," I said. It was

cute the way he was so concerned.

"Glad to hear it," he said, and stopped. I stopped walking too. "Because I sent out the e-mail last night. The experiment can start tomorrow to give people time to participate, but I already got a lot of e-mails back from people saying they'd do it."

"I know. I saw it. That's awesome! Now we need to get some teachers on board. How about you ask your teachers today personally and I'll ask mine? We only need a few anyway, just to have that side of the story."

"Sounds good," Michael said.

"Can you forward me all the replies as they come in?"

"Will do," Michael said, and saluted me. "Can you meet after school in the *Voice* office on Thursday to shape the article? By then we should have enough feedback."

"Sure," I said, and hurried off to class.

Over the next few days, tons of e-mails came in about the twenty-four-hour-text-free day, as we called it. Michael and I participated too. I didn't really find it to be that big a deal. I could still e-mail, message, and call people, so I was shocked at how many people replied saying how hard it was. One girl said, "I couldn't make it through an entire day without texting. I only lasted about ten hours." A guy said, "It was torture. I need some time to zone out and text instead of just constant schoolwork. And suddenly I couldn't do that and had nothing to fill the void."

Some people confessed to why it was so hard to stop. "It's addictive," wrote another girl. "Even though we're not allowed to text during class, I still do. I haven't gotten caught. I text my friends at least twice a period. Usually when the teacher is putting an assignment on the board. But please don't rat on me!"

And we wouldn't. We mentioned in the e-mail that all quotes in the article would be anonymous because we were afraid if we didn't make the experiment a safe place to speak up, people wouldn't want to contribute. Mr. Trigg cleared that with the principal, Mr. Pfeiffer, as well.

I stopped by the *Voice* office to see if I had any new Dear Know-It-All letters for the next issue so I could get a head start, but I could see Jessica Kelly through the little window in the door. I almost didn't go in, but then I saw Michael and Jeff in the back. They were sitting together, looking at the computer. I had wanted to see the photos Jeff had taken of Hailey and me the other day, so I went in.

"Hey, Spilly," Michael said.

Jeff looked at Michael and then at me. "Spilly?" he said.

"Never mind." I glared at Michael and sat down next to them. "Can I see those pictures you took of us the other day?" I asked.

"Sure," Jeff said, clicking on a file. He scrolled down through a lot of photos he had snapped in the hallways and the cafeteria. He passed by one of Hailey.

"Wait a minute!" I said. "There's Hailey. Can I see?"

Jeff clicked on it to enlarge it. She was standing in the hallway by her locker, holding her books. She smiled her typical sparkly smile, but her eyes seemed so blue and her legs were supertan and looked really long and slender. Her hair glowed a golden blond. She looked incredible!

"Jeff," I said. "This is the best picture I've ever seen of Hailey."

"Photoshop!" Jeff responded with a big smile. "I made her legs a little longer and tanner, her hair blonder, her eyes bluer . . . I touched up all of my friends' photos, so they all look fantastic."

"Are you serious?" I said. ***School Paper Photographer Makes Students Unrecognizable.*** This was dangerous territory, wasn't it? I stared at Hailey's photo. It was true. Hailey looked great, but she didn't exactly look like the Hailey I knew. Michael leaned in closer too. I moved my head back. That's all I needed, another head-on collision with Michael Lawrence. "Is that a good idea? I mean it's kind of a lie," I said.

"Oh please," Jeff replied, and waved his hand at me, quickly dismissing what I said. "Who wouldn't want to look better in a photo? Magazines do it all the time."

"Yeah, and then us normal people feel like

we have to live up to expectations that don't even exist! Right, Michael?"

Michael just gave me a blank stare. "Uh, I kind of agree with Jeff. Nobody wants to look bad in a photo. I mean, why not?"

I sighed and sat back in my chair. Once again, I was going to have to agree to disagree with Michael or knock heads, not quite so literally this time.

"Check this out," Jeff said, and pulled up a picture of me at the ice-cream shop. My hair looked smooth and silky. I remember it had just rained that day, so I knew it had actually been frizzier. My skin was glowing and there wasn't any red spot on my chin.

"*Wow!* Great picture, Sam!" Michael said. "Maybe you could e-mail it—," he started to say to Jeff and then stopped. Jeff and I both stared at him. He continued. "I mean, maybe you could keep it on file in case Sam needs a photo for the paper."

Did he just almost ask Jeff to e-mail him the picture? I couldn't help but blush. I did look pretty great. "My hair definitely didn't look like that the other day," I said.

"The magic of the computer! Now, if I were running an article about you in the paper, wouldn't you want me to use this photo instead of *this*?" he asked, and clicked on another photo. It was the un-Photoshopped version, frizzy hair, red spot, and all.

"You look great in both," Michael said. I wondered if he was telling the truth or if he was just saying that because I was right there.

"There isn't a huge difference," I said, but it certainly was tempting to pick the Photoshopped one, even though it didn't totally look like me. "Is there?" I could just pretend for a moment that I looked like a hair model and had flawless skin. Maybe Michael and Jeff were right. Maybe the world was supposed to look a little better on the page. This was something I had to think about.

Chapter 8

NEW EDITOR IN CHIEF WINS MOST-ANNOYING-PERSON AWARD

★ ★ ★

On Thursday at the *Voice* office, Michael and I pulled up our files that we'd saved on the desktop at school and at home. Jessica also backed up everyone's files weekly. Last year we had a near meltdown when we first put the *Voice* online. There was a power outage just before we were going to post our first online issue, and in one split second we lost everything. We were able to cobble together the issue from e-mailed files and our notes, but it was almost disastrous. So ever since then, we all kept duplicate files and a main weekly *Voice* backup. I wondered if Jessica was remembering to do that, but it wasn't really my place to check up on her. Was there a part of me that wanted her to make a mistake? I knew that wasn't right, but the way she acted like she thought she had the responsibility of Mr. Trigg got on my last nerve.

I wrote the lead and started on the "who" and "what" paragraphs. Most articles had to answer the five W's—who, what, where, when, and why— and also how. Michael started playing around with some of the "who" and "where" and inserted our quotes. We had quotes now from a lot of teachers. We were both surprised at how much they wanted to participate, not only in the text-free day, but in the input. My math teacher, Mr. Rinaldi, said that he'd enjoyed the text-free day. "I could use more days without all that beeping and buzzing. It's incredibly distracting, which is why we need rules and limitations for it." Michael's language arts teacher was much more pro-texting and said she was considering integrating text messages into her classroom. "We could set up 'live response' systems. It could add a whole new and exciting level of communication that kids would really respond to."

My favorite was from my science teacher,

Mrs. Fuller. She said, "I don't think texting is bad as long as it's used in productive ways. I could blast-text my students reminders about important tests coming up and due dates. If you can't beat 'em, join 'em! It's an important piece of technology, and it's not going away."

I personally thought she was on the money. Texting definitely wasn't going away. We needed to work together as a school on better ways to use and handle it, instead of just blocking out something that was only going to have a bigger presence in the future.

As Michael and I were busy piecing things together, Jessica Kelly came in and waved hi to me and Michael.

"How's it going?" she asked, coming over. She stopped at our computers and leaned over my shoulder, reading the screen. Susannah, the old editor in chief, never did that. She read our pieces when we sent them to her. It was an unwritten writer code that you never read someone's stuff without asking. I was tempted to cover the screen with my hand. *New Editor in Chief Wins*

Most-Annoying-Person Award. What was she doing? I saw Michael's shoulders stiffen a bit as Jessica read.

"Is that your lead?" she asked, pointing to my first line on the screen.

"Yes," I said. What else would it be? I thought.

"Hmmm," she said, and kept reading.

"What?" I asked, trying not to sound furious, which I was quickly becoming.

"Maybe something with a little more punch?" she said, and then gave what I thought was a fake smile to both of us. "But good work, guys. Keep it coming." She sat down at another computer across the room. Michael and I looked at each other. I made sure she couldn't see me, then rolled my eyes.

"Okay, so . . . where were we?" Michael said in an energetic tone, trying to keep us positive and focused. I decided to type a message to him at the bottom of the page, since she would hear me if I said anything to him.

What is up with her? Is it me, or is she a LOT more annoying than Susannah? I typed really fast, then nudged him so he'd look.

He read it and nodded. **She is**, he wrote. **But she has kept things superorganized. She has half the paper up and edited already. Susannah was always rushing to catch up at the last minute.**

I'd still take S over her any day, I typed, watched him read, and then erased it all, so she'd never see it. I slumped back in my seat and crossed my arms. Yeah, I'll give her a lead with more punch! Michael squeezed my shoulder. I smiled and looked at his blue eyes and relaxed a bit. Maybe Jessica was a pain, but anything that caused a reason for Michael to squeeze my shoulder was fine with me.

"Want to call it quits for now? We can e-mail this to ourselves and work on it at home. I think we have a solid rough draft here," he said. I noticed he looked at Jessica and said "rough draft" just a little extra loud. She kept her eyes glued to her screen and typed fast, as if her life depended on it. "And honestly," Michael now said in almost a whisper, leaning close to me, "this isn't more than a puff piece. We're not babies. We know we're not supposed to text during class. I'm not a big fan of texting, but my older brother Tommy is—so what? He knows enough when to stop."

I ran my fingers through my hair to smooth out any frizzes. I found myself doing that more often since I'd seen Jeff's unretouched photo of me. I knew this article wasn't hard news, but I wouldn't call it a puff piece. "I don't know," I said to Michael. "I feel like the more feedback we get from people, the more it seems like they actually are distracted by texting, both in and out of school. I think it's an important topic to open up."

"I'm kind of ready to be done and move on to other subjects."

I just shrugged. I didn't want to say anything else about it. I wasn't in the mood for an argument. We already had some conflict about the Photoshop issue. Maybe if I added some things into the article to add a little weight to everything, beyond just how people can't stop texting for twenty-four hours, he'd come over to my side.

That night I worked hard on the article and

thought about our conversation. Maybe he was right, but I was surprised he still felt that way, since I found the article becoming only more relevant the deeper I got into it. Why wasn't he having the same experience? How could he not see that texting was a pretty charged issue? I Googled around and tried to find some research that supported my hunch. What came up were tons of articles about the dangers of texting while driving. There were some very scary statistics correlating texting and serious accidents, certainly not something to be taken lightly. There were also lots of statistics about how young adults text more than any other population. I also found out that many schools ban phones altogether because if they're in the building, kids will find a way to sneak texts. Many teachers and administrators said that when kids are texting in the school, they are simply not paying attention. I cited some of this information to add weight to the piece and hoped Michael would see that this was a pretty important topic.

I also gritted my teeth and rewrote my lead,

which now read, *Strict new texting rules at Cherry Valley have put a damper on students' phone usage and mood in recent weeks*, instead of *The administration at Cherry Valley enforced strict texting rules to the dismay of the student body in recent weeks*. I have to admit I liked it better, but I wish Jessica had given us feedback after the whole article was done. I always do a rewrite before I post my article. And the number-one rule for an editor in chief, or anyone who gets to weigh in on my writing—ask first! That's what annoyed me the most. I can take some feedback, especially when it makes the article better. I got up and stretched and walked into the kitchen for some hot chocolate. I took out the milk and chocolate powder and stirred it together. Then I put it in the microwave and waited as the kitchen started to smell sweet and chocolaty.

"Mmmm," Mom said, coming in. "Making hot chocolate?"

"Yeah. You want some?" I asked. The microwave beeped. I took my mug out, being careful that I didn't burn myself. It was really hot, so I poured in a bit more milk and stirred it with my spoon.

"No thanks. I'll just make myself some tea," she said, filling up the teapot with water. "How's it going? You've been closed up in your room all evening."

"Good, actually. I've made a lot of headway on the texting article. I'm surprised how many people could barely last twenty-four-hours without texting. Even some of the teachers!"

Mom leaned against the kitchen counter and crossed her arms. "I can kind of understand that. I remember when I worked without even e-mail. I had to call people on the phone all the time for every question I had. E-mail and texts are certainly convenient, but there was something really nice about hearing people's voices. I also saved up my questions so I'd have one productive phone call. Can you even imagine?" she said, her eyes twinkling with sarcasm.

"Have to say, I can't. But I like calling people sometimes, like when I have to talk something out with Hailey. I don't want to type everything out, you know?"

"I do know," Mom said, pouring herself a steaming cup of tea.

"Michael thinks it's no big deal. At first I thought he was right, but now I'm finding out some really alarming stuff. Not just about how much it can distract you in the classroom, but on the road too."

Mom's eyes widened, and she nodded quickly as she swallowed her tea. "Yes," she said when she finally swallowed. "I never wanted to tell you this, but about two years ago I got a ticket for using my phone in the car. I wasn't texting, just talking to someone. But that's the last time I ever did that. It was a really stupid thing to do, and I'm glad I got a ticket. Maybe it's good I'm telling you this so you know how serious it is. It probably saved me from getting into an accident."

Whoa. Hold the phone. *Girl Finds Out Mother Can Be Just as Stupid as Teenagers.* I swallowed hard. It was scary to think of Mom doing something dangerous on the road.

"I'm glad you told me. And I'm glad you don't do that anymore."

"I don't, and I hope you and Allie will get how dangerous it is to use the phone while driving. I've drilled it into your sister's head a million times since she started driving, but let me know if you ever see her do it. That'll be a time when it's okay to tattle."

"That won't be a problem," I said, grinning. I finished my hot chocolate and went back into my room. I had a lot of energy. Working on the article had charged me up and it was only nine o'clock. I thought about messaging Hailey, but after the talk with Mom, I was in the mood to actually hear her voice. I went to the den, curled up on the couch, and dialed the phone.

"Are you okay?" she said when she got on the phone.

"Yeah, sorry to call so late," I said, and wondered if I should have texted or messaged her instead.

"No, no. I'm up, barely," she said, and yawned. Hailey was more of a morning person.

Me, I usually got a second wind after nine. But then I wasn't happy in the morning.

"So I saw this fantastic photo of you that Jeff took," I said, stretching my legs out on the couch, knowing that bit of information would perk her right up.

"Really? At the ice-cream shop?" she said, her voice lifting.

"Well, those were good. But there was one he took of you in the hallway and it is a really good picture, but he made it extra good."

"What do you mean?" Hailey asked.

"He touched it up with Photoshop," I replied.

"Oh," she said, and paused. Then she continued. "That's kind of weird." She lowered her voice as if someone else were listening to her. "So how good do I look?"

"Ha!" I cried. "This from a person who's always telling me to stop worrying about my hair. And I have pretty good hair. I thought you didn't really care how you look."

"Of course I care how I look—I just don't want to waste hours every day fiddling around with makeup and clothes, you know? I have more important things to do. But if someone makes me look extra great and I didn't even have to do anything, now, that I wanna see."

I laughed. "You're one of a kind, Hailey!"

"Yeah, especially Photoshopped."

"No," I said, now serious. "Not the Photoshopped version. The real Hailey is my favorite version," I said, and I meant it. "You know, Jeff did one of me too, and I have to say, I looked pretty awesome, especially my hair."

"See? You loved it," Hailey said.

"Well yeah, I do look good in a weird sort of way. And guess what? I think Michael almost asked Jeff for a copy in front of me." I cleared my throat. "The Photoshopped version. Not the other one."

"Interesting. Well, the good side is that at least he wanted a photo of you looking extra fine," Hailey said. "Can't blame him for that."

"I guess not," I responded, but I still wasn't sure if I liked this whole idea of Photoshopping school newspaper photos. It didn't feel, well, honest. What would Hailey think if I gave her a photo of Frank with his ears shrunk and his hair lightened? If she thought the picture was cute, it wouldn't matter, because that's not who he really was. As I said in my Dear Know-It-All letter, *If he asks you to cut your hair, he doesn't make the cut.*

Was this like Michael wanting me to cut my hair, so to speak?

Chapter 9

REPORTER FINALLY ADMITS DEFEAT!

★ ★ ★

Amazingly, I didn't have any homework for the weekend and took a break from the paper. The article was basically done ahead of schedule, and Mr. Trigg had approved the Dear Know-It-All letter. I was trying to remember to take breaks and have more fun this year. Last year, things got so busy sometimes and I got too stressed out, certainly more stressed out than a girl my age should be!

Mom, Allie, and I went out for Chinese food on Friday night. And Hailey slept over on Saturday. We spent the evening scoping around Buddybook, baking totally nonvegan cupcakes, and watching a movie.

"See, I would just shave a little off the ears and make him a touch taller," Hailey said as we checked out a cute picture of Frank playing baseball.

"Now you want him taller? You're impossible!" I exclaimed. "How would you like it if he and Michael were doing the same thing in their rooms tonight?"

"Well," said Hailey, looking carefully at the screen. "See right there." She pointed at a list of names on the right. "Frank and Michael are both on Buddybook right now, so they just might be."

"You can see that?" I said, leaning in to look at the list.

"Yup," she said. "How much do I have to pay you to join the modern world and open a Buddybook account?"

"A million dollars. I already tried that and it's not for me. I'll just stick with e-mailing and texting, thank you very much." I got up from my chair. When I'd joined Buddybook, I'd gotten completely obsessed with it and it had made me distracted and insecure. Not for me. "Close it out. The whole thing's making me nervous right now, like they can see us."

Hailey bent her head down and started laughing hysterically. "Yeah, they can see us through the peephole in the computer," she said between giggles.

I picked up a pillow from my bed. "Oh, you think that's funny?" I took a little whack at her with the pillow.

She whipped around in her chair and got up. "Are you sure you want to mess with a star athlete, Martone?" Hailey said. She picked up a pillow and whacked me good. I held my ground and didn't fall.

"Yeah, let me see what you got." I whacked her harder. Hailey centered herself and whacked me back again, this time really hard. I fell, but kind of into Hailey, and she came tumbling down on top of me. We were a heap of laughing arms, legs, and pillows. Then we both lay back on the floor, trying to catch our breath, the giggles still coming. A perfect Saturday night, if you ask me.

Monday came way too fast. I shuffled down the hallway at school to my first class, trying to feel awake.

"Sam," Michael called out behind me.

"Oh, hey," I said, and smiled. Sometimes when I hadn't seen Michael in a few days, I realized that I had missed him—not that I would ever tell him that in a hundred years.

He smiled at me meekly and quickly looked down again.

"Is something wrong?" I asked. He seemed a little uncomfortable, not himself.

"I thought about the texting article, how I said it was a puff piece. It's not. You're right."

Reporter Finally Admits Defeat! "I'm sorry," I said, grinning. "I couldn't quite hear you. Can you say that again?"

He gave me a weak smile. "You're right."

"I still couldn't quite make out what you said," I joked, cupping my hand to my ear and squinting my eyes.

"Okay, I gotta go. Talk to you later," Michael said quickly, and walked away. I swallowed hard, my cheeks on fire with embarrassment. I hoped he knew I was just joking. Had I offended him? It was not like Michael to be so serious. Usually, I was the one who was too serious.

"Did you just see a ghost?" Hailey came bounding up to me, holding her backpack tight around her shoulders. My shoulders relaxed on seeing her.

"No," I said, shaking my head. "I think I just went too far."

"Went too far where? With who? Catch me up here a little," Hailey said, eyes widening with curiosity.

I took in a deep breath and let it out slowly to steady myself. "Michael just came up and told me I was right to take the texting article more seriously than he did. So I joked that I couldn't hear him so he'd say I was right again, because, um, you know how often that happens," I said.

"Yeah, and?" Hailey said, circling her hand for me to continue.

"So he said it," I continued, feeling sort of out of breath. "But then I joked again about it, and he just kind of walked away and barely cracked a smile. Do you think I was being obnoxious?"

"No more than usual," she said, smiling.

"Now you're being obnoxious," I said back, annoyed. This wasn't time for joking anymore.

I was suddenly afraid I had really upset Michael when I was just trying to be funny. I felt awful.

"Chillax, girl" Hailey said. "I was just joking with *you*!"

"I know," I said, hanging my head. "I'm just worried."

Hailey put her arm around me. "Michael does not think you're obnoxious. Maybe he just had something else on his mind. I think you're way overreacting."

I looked up and shrugged. "I hope you're right."

All morning I was counting the minutes to lunch, but I was also really nervous to see Michael again. I got to the cafeteria early because I thought it was better if he saw me first than if I saw him first. If he came up to me, I'd know things were okay, and if he ignored me, then I'd just sit tight and let Hailey console me.

There weren't that many people in the cafeteria. I got a tray and chose a chicken, avocado, and cheddar melt on whole-grain bread from the organic-option table. At least I'd have a good lunch. I was starving.

I walked to the tables with my tray and saw
Jessica Kelly sitting at a table by herself with a
stack of paper in front of her, gripping a pencil. I
didn't want to deal with her right now, so I started
to turn away.

"Sam," she called. I stopped midturn and
glanced at her.

"Oh, hi, Jessica," I said a little too sweetly,
acting as if I were surprised to see her.

"Hi, um, want to sit here?" She pointed to a
chair near her with her pencil, seeming unusually
friendly.

I looked around for a second. This wasn't
what I'd had planned for my lunch hour. What if
Michael walked in and sat down before I could
even see if he noticed me? What if Jessica started
giving me a list of pointers on my article that I
never asked for?

"I mean, if you were planning to sit somewhere
else, that's okay. I just wanted to ask you a question," she said in a small voice. I studied her face
for a second. She looked a little pale and tired.

"Oh no. I can sit here," I said. She was being

so nice, I now felt a little bad that I had planned to ditch her.

I put my tray on the table and sat down. "What's up?" I asked cheerfully, trying to keep the mood light, but inside my stomach was churning. Between being on the lookout for Michael and now wondering what Jessica was going to ask me, it was a little more than I could take.

She put her head in her hands and made a little moaning sound.

"Jessica? You okay?" I asked, now worrying that everyone I knew had been replaced by imposters.

"No," she said, lifting her head. "I had no idea that the paper was going to take over my life like this. I have to make sure everything is perfect for the first issue, and I only have three more days to do it. I've been trying to keep up with everything, but now I'm afraid I'm going to overlook a million things and the paper will be the laughingstock of the school." The words tumbled out, her face growing redder and redder, as if she might even cry.

Wait, what? ***Tough Editor in Chief Has a Weak Spot.*** I had no idea Jessica felt like this! She seemed so organized and sure of herself, annoyingly so. I thought I was the stress monster, making sure everything was perfect, doing draft after draft. But I knew that if I were editor in chief, I wouldn't have the time to go over every single word. That's what the section editors were for, and Mr. Trigg was great at looking at the paper as a whole. Also, most reporters were pretty seasoned, like me and Michael. We took fact checking and proofreading seriously, and Susannah had always relied on us for that. She never proofread the whole paper.

"I think you might be trying to do too much," I said as nicely as I could.

"Like I have a choice!" Jessica said, stiffening.

I wanted to back down, but I also wanted to help her. I definitely did not want to argue with her, though. That was the last thing I needed right now, issues with the editor in chief. I already had enough drama going on.

"It's okay if you don't want my advice, but I

just want to see if I can help you. Honestly, I do," I said softly.

She relaxed her shoulders, sat back in her chair, and crossed her arms. "Okay. Give me what you've got."

I sat up a little taller. "Well, as a former reporter, you're probably used to focusing really hard on your article. But when you're editor in chief, you can't have that kind of focus on each article. Leave that to the reporters and the section editors. Your job is just to make sure everything flows and gets in on time. And you're doing a great job," I forced myself to say. She was, in some ways. She obviously really needed to hear it. I took it a step further and hoped I wouldn't regret it. "Don't tell her I said this, and I love Susannah, but you're more organized than she was."

"Really?" Jessica said, finally a smile spreading over her face.

"Totally. The paper's going to be fine."

She frowned. "Just fine?"

Good grief. I had no idea Jessica Kelly was so insecure. She wasn't who I thought she was at all.

"It'll be fantastic!" I said, and patted her on the shoulder. She brightened.

"Thanks, Sam. I needed to hear that. And I really liked your new lead on the texting article."

"Oh, good. Glad you liked it," I said, and returned the smile. She must have felt really alone. I probably would have, too, on my first issue as editor in chief. For the first time, I was glad that it wasn't me. I liked being able to roll my sleeves up and really get into a story. It was lonely at the top. Hopefully, now she'd be a little more easygoing in the *Voice* office.

Oh no! I thought, looking around. I had been so wrapped up with giving Jessica a pep talk I hadn't even noticed if Michael had walked in the cafeteria or not.

"Something wrong?" Jessica asked.

"What? No, no, it's nothing. Just, um, wondering if Hailey was here," I said distractedly. I scanned the room. There he was! I saw him sitting at a table with a bunch of guys on the football team, though kind of off to the side. He didn't really look like he was participating in the conversation. I guess he was still in a mood. If he'd seen me, he probably hadn't wanted to come anywhere near me since I was sitting with Jessica.

"Do you mind if I keep working?" Jessica said, her editor in chief persona returning.

"Go ahead. Want me to look at anything?"

"Sure, if you're up for it! Could you just check this for errors?" she said, beaming, and handed me the sports section. I started reading through it, but my mind was racing. Well, I wasn't about to go over and plop myself in the middle of that group anyway. I think I just needed to let this one breathe. Everyone had insecurities. But I'd been obsessing over mine so much lately, between the Photoshopped picture of me, Michael saying he thought Allie would look good with short hair, and now my joking with him. Michael and I always joked around with each other. This was no different. I was tired of feeling insecure and worrying about every little thing. If he was upset by it, then he was responsible for dealing with his own feelings. So there. I had work to do.

Chapter 10

BOY MYSTERIOUSLY KEEPS TERRIBLE SECRET

★ ★ ★

"Where were you all day?" Hailey asked me, a little out of breath while I was loading up my bag with books to take home that afternoon. I had so much homework, I could scream. Thank goodness, at least the paper was almost put to bed, as they say in the journalism world.

"Where were you? I didn't even see you at lunch," I replied.

"Sorry. I hid in the library, cramming for a science quiz," Hailey said.

Normally I might be hurt that she hadn't asked for my help, but secure Sam took a moment. Maybe she just thought she could focus better alone. I certainly knew how that felt.

"But," she said, her eyes practically popping out of her head, "did you hear what happened to Michael's brother Tommy?"

My heart started to beat really fast. "No. What happened?"

"He was in a car accident. I saw Frank in the library and he told me," Hailey said quickly.

"Oh my gosh. Was he hurt?"

"Not really, but I guess he could have been. And guess what?" she said, still wide-eyed and breathless.

"What?" I wasn't even sure if I wanted to know. I felt a little shaky all over. Poor Michael. That's probably why he was upset today. It had nothing to do with me.

"The reason he got into the accident was because he was"—she paused for a moment—"texting."

Her words hit me like a rock. *Boy Mysteriously Keeps Terrible Secret.* I couldn't say anything. I really wanted to talk to Michael. My joke must have seemed so awful to him, but how could I have known? Why hadn't he told me?

"Sam?" Hailey asked, worried.

"Yeah, I'm just in a little bit of shock. What a terrible thing to have happened now. I need to talk to Michael," I said. He must be feeling pretty bad right now, since he was the one who had dismissed the seriousness of the article in the first place.

"I saw him by his locker earlier," Hailey said.

"Okay. I'll call you later." I picked up my bag. Hailey nodded.

I walked as fast as I could down one hallway and down another to get to Michael's locker, but he was nowhere to be seen. I did see Frank up ahead.

"Frank," I called out. "Have you seen Michael? Hailey told me what happened."

"Yeah, I think he's on his way home," he said.

"Is he okay?" I asked.

"Yeah, just shaken up. But Tommy's fine," Frank replied.

"Okay, I'm going to try and catch up with him." I hurried toward the main school doors.

I ran out the doors and squinted into the late-afternoon sun. Way up ahead, I saw Michael heading off toward his house. I took a deep breath.

"Michael!" I yelled. A few kids turned around, but I didn't care what anyone thought of me. I just wanted to make things right with Michael. He didn't turn around. This time I yelled his name even louder. He stopped and turned around, scanning the crowd of students and buses. I ran toward him, waving my hand. He caught my eye and smiled. That was a good sign.

"Hey, Sam. Are you okay?" he called out to me, looking concerned.

I stopped to catch my breath. "I"—I took another breath—"heard"—breath—"about what happened to Tommy," I finally managed to get out.

"Is that why you came running after me? I thought all the *Voice* office computers exploded or something!" he said, grinning.

"No, I was worried about you. And I felt really stupid about joking with you this morning," I said, looking down at my feet.

"Hey." Michael put his hand on my shoulder. I felt its warmth and wanted to just melt right there on the sidewalk. "You didn't know. I was just really distracted. I didn't mean to act so upset. I mean, I was, but not about your joke," he explained.

"Oh, good," I said, feeling incredibly relieved. "So what happened, exactly? I heard about it from Hailey who heard about it from Frank, but I didn't get the whole story."

This time Michael took a deep breath. His face went from happy to serious. "Well, Tommy had just pulled out of the driveway and at the same time got a text from his girlfriend. He took his eyes off the road for a second and swerved, hitting a parked car on the street."

"Oh my gosh!" I said.

"And . . . the parked car happened to be my dad's. I've never seen my dad so mad. They took away his driving privileges, like, indefinitely."

"They should have!" I exclaimed. "It could have been so much worse."

"I know," he said, nodding. "Tommy was really shaken up too. It's amazing that one split second can change things. We're really lucky he wasn't hurt and he didn't hurt anyone else."

"I'm sorry it happened at all. It's kind of

strange that it happened now," I said, hoping that was okay to point out.

"Yeah. I can't stop thinking about it. All along, I was thinking that getting distracted by texting was no big deal. I feel like I need to write about it."

"You mean for the paper?" I asked.

"Yeah, like a sidebar to the main article. I'm planning to talk to Mr. Trigg tomorrow."

"You absolutely should," I agreed.

At the *Voice* office the next day, I went with Michael to talk to Mr. Trigg about the sidebar.

"I think that sounds brilliant," Mr. Trigg said. "But we'll need it by Thursday. The paper goes up Friday. Can you write it that fast?"

Michael nodded. "I know exactly what I want to write."

"Give it a go, then. It sounds like you've got something important to say."

While Michael started drafting his piece, I went over to Jeff's computer and checked out what he was working on.

"Wow," I said, also taking a look at some of the

photos he was uploading into our article.

"You like?" he said, turning around to face me, a big smile on his face.

"Don't get me wrong. It looks great. But I can barely recognize anyone. This is not a fashion magazine. And even then, I think those magazines go way overboard," I said, hoping I wouldn't hurt Jeff's feelings. Still, I had to say it.

"So looking like an upscale magazine is a bad thing?" Jeff scoffed, immediately getting defensive.

"Well, yeah, since that's not what we are," I said back at him, hands on my hips.

"I'll bet if you brought any of these people in here, they'd all rather look a little better than a little worse," Jeff replied.

"Jeff, that's not the point. I was just—," I started to say, but Mr. Trigg interrupted.

"What's all the hullabaloo?" he asked, throwing his scarf over his shoulder.

Jeff and I glared at each other.

"Jeff has Photoshopped all the pictures in our texting article! He's literally changed the way people look. I thought we were supposed to be covering reality here." My emotions were starting to get the better of me.

"I'm just doing what people do. We have the technology. I don't get why you don't want people to look better," he said, turning to me.

"That's just your opinion. I think people look fine the way they really are," I shot back, my voice becoming louder and shrill.

"Okay, okay. Take a breather, folks," Mr. Trigg said, putting his hands on our shoulders like a referee in a boxing match. "Jeff," he went on, looking at him square in the eye. "I admire your Photoshop talents, but I must admit that I agree with Ms. Martone on this one. We're a newspaper. We let people make up their own minds and opinions. That's the difference. We are not a beauty magazine pushing a certain image here. We're just running photos of the kids in the story. Now, I don't believe in running purposefully unflattering pictures—that's another kind of journalism. But we need to run photos that are an accurate representation of the students."

"Okay, but what about this guy?" Jeff showed us a picture of a student with a big smear of what looked like pizza sauce on his mouth. "Are you saying I shouldn't touch up anything?"

"No," I said, a little calmer now. "I think that falls into what Mr. Trigg said about purposefully publishing unflattering pictures. I think it's okay to fix something like that and just make him look like he normally does."

"You're on the money, Martone," Mr. Trigg said. "Let's try to stick with those principles."

Jeff sighed and nodded. "Okay. I guess I get it. I don't *like* it, but I get it."

I was thankful that Mr. Trigg had been there to take my side before Jeff turned the *Voice* into *Vogue*. Before I left, I stopped over at Michael's computer. He was totally lost in thought, writing his piece, typing away. I didn't want to disturb him, but I wanted to say good-bye. I leaned over and said in a low voice, "Catch you later, Mikey."

He jumped when he heard me, and his notebook, which was on his lap, fell to the floor. Out slipped a photo . . . of me. Not just any old photo either—the Photoshopped version that Jeff had taken in the ice-cream shop! I stared at it, my mouth dropping open. Michael stared at it too for a second before grabbing it.

"That's weird," he said, nervously looking at the photo like he'd never seen it before. I noticed his cheeks were growing a little red. "I don't know how that ended up in my notebook. It must have gotten mixed up with my things when I was working with Jeff." He still kept his eyes on the photo instead of me.

"Huh," I said. "Weird."

"I'll give it back to him after I'm done with this article," he continued. Then he slipped the photo back into his notebook and turned his attention to the computer screen.

"Okay, I'll let you work," I responded in a perky way, trying to pretend what just happened hadn't totally freaked me out. *Boy Likes Photo Better Than Actual Girl* is what came to mind.

As I left, I saw Jessica sitting with Mr. Trigg, going over the paper on-screen. She was smiling and looked much more relaxed than I had ever seen her. She caught my eye as I left and gave me a thumbs-up. I gave her one back. I was glad I had told her what I really thought. If I hadn't felt confident enough to do it, she might not have heard what she needed to hear and would still be stressing out over every little word and driving us all crazy. One major thing being Dear Know-It-All has taught me is not to be afraid to say what I think. Most of the time, even with my sometimes frizzy hair and less-than-perfect skin, I thought being me, the *real* me, as in the un-Photoshopped version of me, was pretty cool. I just hoped Michael thought that, too.

Chapter 11

TO CRUSH OR NOT TO CRUSH?

★ ★ ★

"He had it in his notebook!" Hailey cried, her eyes bugging out while we both shared a bowl of popcorn at my house after school.

"Mmm-hmm." I nodded vigorously, my mouth full.

"I think this is a good thing," she stated, pointing one finger in the air.

"Yeah? Why? It means that he'd rather me be all model-perfect-looking instead of the way I really look. Just like you wish Frank looked different. Then you would like him. Ugh! I'm Michael's Frank!" I wailed, putting my head down on the counter. *To Crush or Not to Crush?* That was the question.

"No way!" Hailey said. "Not at all. I do not carry a Photoshopped version of Frank around. I would never want to."

I lifted up my head from the kitchen counter. "Really? Why?"

"Because the reason that I don't have a crush on Frank is because I just don't. His ears might be a little big and he might not be totally my taste, but crushes are more mysterious than that. Frank's a great guy, but you just like who you like, and when you like someone, they appear more perfect than they really are. If anyone knows that, you do. That picture," Hailey said, pointing to a spot on the counter as if the picture were there, "is probably the way he actually does see you. That's why he likes it! He probably sleeps with it under his pillow," she said.

"Oh, stop," I said, nudging her in the shoulder. "Maybe you're right," I said, shrugging.

"Right about what?" Allie came padding into the kitchen in her bare feet, her hair up in a towel, some yellowish gooey gunk covering her whole face.

"Nothing," I said. "And *what* is all over your face?"

"A soy milk, honey, and cinnamon mask."

"You've really gone over the edge now," I said. ***Older Sister Might Actually Be Alien.***

"What does that do?" Hailey asked, actually curious.

"Oh my gosh," Allie said, excitedly coming over to Hailey. "It makes your skin look as smooth and creamy as, well, soy milk! It's incredible."

"Oooh, can I try some?" Hailey said, clapping her hands.

"Sure! Both of you get towels. I'll whip up more mask and we'll have a little spa afternoon!"

I sighed. I guess it couldn't hurt. Maybe a soy milk and honey mask would make me look more like Jeff's photo. Not that I wanted to, not really.

Friday morning, the paper came out. The online version of the paper gets posted early, before people get the hard copy at school. There were already fifty comments online when I checked in the morning. I was psyched that it was generating a lot of buzz. I had to rush to school, so I didn't have time to read Michael's sidebar yet. The moment I got there, I grabbed a copy of the paper and sat down by my locker. I scanned our article and was pleased to see the photographs looking like normal, real people. Then I read his article:

A Lesson Learned

By Michael Lawrence

My older brother Tommy did something really stupid, and it could have cost him his life or someone else's. Because of a text message. He was driving to pick up his girlfriend when she texted him and asked, "Where r u? We're going 2b late." He took his eyes off the road for one second to text back, "Don't worry. I'm on my way." That might have been the last thing he ever wrote.

He swerved and hit my father's car, parked on the side of the road. Thankfully, he wasn't hurt, though there was significant damage to both cars. He hadn't been driving fast and had barely even gotten on the road. After the accident, he said, "I always knew I would never text on a main road or a highway, but I thought, I'm just starting out. I'm going really slow. It's fine. It wasn't fine. What if someone had been walking near the car or had been coming the other way? I feel lucky that nothing worse happened."

None of us want to think about that, but we have to. This has forced me to understand that texting, though a convenient way of communicating, must be done responsibly. It is a major source of distraction and not just while driving, but while doing anything else. If I'm texting, I'm not listening to my teacher or to my friends. It can really bug people sometimes. It can even be dangerous while walking, especially if you're crossing the street.

Before Samantha Martone and I started writing our article, I have to admit, I didn't think it was a big enough deal for a whole article. I thought everyone was overreacting, including the school administration with the new no-texting policy. Now I understand that there's a time and a place for texting, and in school or on the road is not where it belongs. Most of all, I'm thankful that Tommy's mistake resulted in an important lesson for all of us, instead of a tragedy.

I sat back and took in a deep breath. I had tears in my eyes. I was blown away. I had never read anything from Michael that was so heartfelt and vulnerable. I was so proud of him.

Hailey suddenly appeared, standing over me.

"Did you read it?"

"Yes," I said. "It was amazing."

"I know. I think it will really change a lot of people's behavior for the better," she said. "I hadn't even thought about it on this kind of level." She smiled. "Both pieces work together really nicely."

"Thanks," I said. "But Michael really took a risk here, and I hope he's recognized for that."

Hailey nodded. "I'm sure he will be."

My worry that Michael would be not be given enough credit for his article was unfounded. Several people came up to *me* and told me what a great piece it was. I kind of liked that people linked us together so much so that they assumed what they said to me would get to Michael. And secure Sam was happy about all the attention her good friend was getting for his good work.

I finally saw Michael at lunch and held up my hand for a high-five. "Nice work, Mikey." I hit his hand hard and gave him a pat on the back.

"Thanks, Pasty," he said, grinning. "Couldn't have done it without you. You really understood the seriousness of it all along. I should have listened sooner." He looked down at his feet.

"Hey," I said gently. "No one knew quite what the stakes were until the thing with Tommy happened. As you said, thank goodness it just proved to be a lesson learned."

Michael nodded gravely.

"Awesome work!" Jessica Kelly came up to us and hugged me out of nowhere. Then she hugged Michael. Never in my wildest dreams did I think Michael and I would get hugs from Jessica. "You guys rock. I'm so glad I get to have writers like you working on the paper. Michael, I was really touched by your sidebar. It was brave of you to write."

"Thanks," said Michael, a hint of red starting to spread on his cheeks. "Just said what I felt."

"The paper looks great," I said. "We should be hugging you for all the hard work you put in."

"Yeah," said Michael. "You knocked it out of the park."

"Really?" Jessica said, smiling from ear to ear, looking back and forth at both of us almost as if she didn't believe what Michael said.

"Really," I said, and I meant it. Jessica wasn't

so bad once she felt better about herself. I liked secure Jessica.

In the afternoon, as Michael and I headed toward the *Voice* office for a post-paper meeting, Mr. Pfeiffer stopped us.

"Michael," he said. "May I speak with you?" I held my breath. Was Mr. Pfeiffer upset with us about the article for some reason? I wasn't sure why he would be, because, in the end, especially with Michael's sidebar, we supported the new texting rules.

"Samantha, you can come too," he said, and started walking. Michael and I looked at each other. He opened his eyes wide, I bit my lip, and we followed Mr. Pfeiffer like little ducks to his office. When we got there, he turned to us and pointed at a framed picture hanging on the hallway wall right outside his door. As I looked closer, I realized that it was a framed copy of Michael's article!

"This may be the most important article you'll ever write. This is the kind of statement that saves lives. My hat is off to you, Mr. Lawrence,"

Mr. Pfeiffer said, and tipped his imaginary hat toward Michael. "And, Samantha, you both did a wonderful job covering this issue. We are looking into some positive ways we can incorporate texting in the classroom."

"Wow, thank you, Mr. Pfeiffer," Michael said. "That means a lot. I just wanted to make sure no one makes the same mistake Tommy did."

"An admirable mission," he said.

"I'm glad you liked our article," I said. "I learned a lot from writing it."

"So did I," Mr. Pfeiffer said. "I have to pop in my office for a bit, but I just wanted to take this moment to recognize your efforts. We're lucky to have you both at this school," he said, and walked into his office.

Michael and I stared at each other in surprise. I had not expected that kind of reaction. I felt proud and happy for Michael that he did get the recognition he deserved for speaking out honestly.

"Just another day at Cherry Valley," Michael said, and shrugged, but there was a little gleam in his eye.

"Yeah! I'll say," I said, and we walked over to the *Voice* office together. Jeff was there, fidgeting around with Photoshop.

"Who are you 'fixing' now?" I asked, smiling.

"Ha-ha," Jeff said. "By the way, man," he said to Michael, "awesome piece." Then he punched him lightly in the shoulder.

"Thanks," Michael said, beaming.

"Okay," Jeff said, getting up and grabbing his camera. "Let me take a picture before you guys are famous reporters at the *New York Times*. Then I'll have proof I knew you when." He motioned for us to stand close together.

Michael moved closer and put his arm around me. I could smell the Tide scent on his shirt. This was turning into the best day ever.

"Smile!" Jeff called, and snapped the photo.

Afterward, we looked at it. It was a nice photo. We both looked happy and relaxed and exactly like *us*, including the faint red spot I still had on my chin.

"That's a great picture," said Michael. "Can I have a copy?"

Jeff and I both looked at him.

He stiffened nervously. "I mean . . . it's for . . . well, we should have one in case we ever need to run a photo of us with one of our stories. Besides, I like this picture of you better than the other one. This one looks like you."

A big smile spread across my face. It was exactly what I needed to hear. It's nice to be confident and be yourself no matter what, but sometimes it doesn't hurt to have a little reinforcement.

"Ah, sure thing," Jeff said, smirking at Michael. "I'll e-mail you both a copy. No touchups, I promise. It's like Know-It-All even said in the column . . . don't change anything for anyone but yourself."

"Yeah, that was a good column," said Michael, looking at me. I'm always paranoid that he knows Dear Know-It-All is me. "It was good last year, but it's just as good this year, don't you think?"

"Um . . . yeah," I said. "I mean, it's the first one, though. Gotta see what happens, right?"

That night I got into my favorite green and black polka-dot p.j.'s and headed off to bed early.

The excitement of the day had exhausted me. I checked my e-mail before getting tucked in. Jeff had e-mailed the photo as promised. I clicked on it, and our smiling faces filled the screen. It made me happy to look at it. I decided to print it out. As it was printing, I texted Michael.

Again, gr8 story!

Thx! Hope u aren't doing anything where u could be distracted! he texted back right away.

Nope, I texted back. Ready 4 bed. Sweet dreams . . .

I hit send, and after I heard the little whooshing signal on the phone that it had been sent off into the ether, I panicked. I read it again. Did I just tell Michael Lawrence sweet dreams? The excitement of the day had really messed with my brain. How embarrassing. But before I could obsess too much about it, I heard a *bing* on my phone.

You 2 Pasty, he wrote back. Sweet dreams. I breathed a sigh of relief and settled into bed, still holding the phone, looking at the text. That Michael, he always managed to surprise me just when I thought I had made a total fool of myself.

There was a knock on the door.

"Yeah," I said, a little startled.

Mom opened the door and came in. "Samantha, I thought you were going to bed early. You still have the lights on, and you aren't supposed to have your phone in your room while you're sleeping," she said sternly, and held out her hand for the phone.

"Sorry, Mom," I said, quickly clicking out of my text window and turning the phone off so she wouldn't see my little interchange. "Here." I handed her the phone. "It won't happen again."

"Riiiight," Mom said doubtfully. "Want to bet money on it? Okay, good night, sweetie. Get some rest." She kissed me on the forehead, turned off the light, and left the room. "Sweet dreams," she called.

Sometimes, I thought as I pulled up the covers, texting *can* really distract you! I thought about everything that had happened in the past week. I'd written a pretty good first Dear Know-It-All column. I'd written a good first story with Michael Lawrence. And, as always, I'd learned a lot.

Texting has both pros and cons. It can be really distracting and, well, not to be dramatic, deadly. But it has its pros too. Like getting a text from the boy you think is the greatest right before you go to sleep.

I smiled and snuggled in as I felt my eyes begin to flutter closed. Sweet dreams, indeed!

Extra! Extra!

Want the scoop on what Samantha is up to next?

Here's a sneak peek of the ninth book in the Dear Know-It-All series:

Cast Your Ballot!

POLLS A PROVING GROUND FOR RISING STAR REPORTER

It is election season at Cherry Valley Middle School, and I cannot wait to cover it for our school newspaper, the *Cherry Valley Voice*. Everyone pays attention to the news around election time, so I'm really psyched to be in the middle of it. Plus, it's good training ground for when I get older and am a star reporter covering the presidential election somewhere. (Watch for me!) I am obsessed with journalism and have spent years reading posts, blogs, newspapers, and magazines and watching coverage of real elections on TV, and I am *ready* to get in there and do it myself! I can just see the headline: **Polls a Proving Ground for Rising Star Reporter**.

Elections have it all: person-on-the-street interviews, polls, background digging, daily highs and lows, analysis—the best stuff journalism has to offer. And what's great is I'll get to do it all—and under my own byline, Sam Martone. Oh, along with that of my writing partner and the crush-of-my-life, Michael Lawrence. Michael and I make a good writing team. Luckily, the paper's faculty supervisor, Mr. Trigg, agrees, so he partners us up for most stories. I have to say, we do make a great pair.

Today Mr. Trigg announced in our newspaper staff meeting that we'd begin election coverage for the next issue. Everyone began whispering with their neighbor (Michael was late, as usual, so I didn't have a neighbor to whisper with at that exact moment), and Mr. Trigg had to call us all to order again.

"Wonderful enthusiasm here today!" He chuckled. "Nothing like an election to get the journalistic juices flowing! All right, then, let's talk assignments. Nikil Gupta and Niall Carey, how about a piece on the election process here at Cherry Valley Middle? Let's focus on: How do people get nominated? How do the campaigns work? Where and how do we vote?"

Mr. Trigg looked at his notes, and just then,

Michael entered with a sheepish grin. He nodded at Mr. Trigg apologetically and quickly joined me on the love seat just inside the newsroom door. I always grab this seat early and save him the other half—it's the best seat for late arrivals, which is what Michael always is. Plus, it *is* called a *love* seat, right? Swoon!

"Ah, Mr. Lawrence. So glad you could join us today," said Mr. Trigg, peering at Michael over his reading glasses. Michael is one of Mr. Trigg's favorites since he's an amazing writer and has a photographic memory, so Mr. Trigg lets Michael get away with a lot of other stuff, like lateness. "I'd like you and Ms. Martone to do profiles of the candidates for school president. Front-page stories. Lots of background, person-on-the-street, and primary interviews with the candidates. Okay, you two?"

He looked at us, and we nodded vigorously and smiled. This was a plum assignment. It would be fun to research and write, and we'd get to work together, which wasn't always a given. I was ecstatic.

"The two candidates are John Scott and . . ." He looked down at his notes. "It's here somewhere . . . hiding . . . I wouldn't want to be running against John Scott either! Oh, here it is! Anthony Wright. Okay?"

"Got it," I said, writing their names down in my trusty notebook even though of course I knew already. I had been reading a lot of posts and paying attention for weeks already about who was running.

"Good note-taking, Pasty," whispered Michael.

I nodded, happy enough to ignore his nickname for me for the millionth time, as well as the fact that he always teases me for writing things down in my notebook.

Mr. Trigg continued. "Let us all remember, reporters, that we are impartial. As the press, we merely reflect what the public says, and we strive to be the ultimate in fair and accurate reporting, especially when it comes to elections. Now, opinion pieces are a different matter, but I don't know that we'll be using them this time around. Feelings *do* get hurt," said Mr. Trigg, rolling his eyes heavenward. "In the words of the late, great Winston Churchill, 'There is no such thing as public opinion. There is only published opinion.' Too true, dear Winston, too true," he said, shaking his head sadly.

Everyone giggled, since Mr. Trigg has this unbelievable ability to find the perfect Churchill quotation for anything. Everyone makes bets on how many times Trigger will mention Churchill in a meeting. Some kids even think he makes the quotations up. I always write them down because I like them, so I'm here to say they're all real because I've Googled them! I actually think they'd make a great article one day.

After the meeting Michael and I both had to run to classes, but we made a plan to meet up later and brainstorm.

"Who are you voting for, by the way?" he asked, a twinkle in his eye.

"I am a journalist! I am objective!" I said indignantly. "I won't know until I have all the facts and can make an informed decision!"

"Innocent until proven guilty, then?" he teased with that adorable smile of his.

"Of course," I huffed, but I smiled back. How could I not?

At lunch, I ate with my best friend, Hailey Jones, and our friends Kristen and Jenna. We are going to the movies this Friday and out for pizza at Slices, and we wanted to talk about which movie to see.

"Action is where it's at, my friends," declared Hailey. She wanted us to go see a movie about a spaceship that loses control or something.

"Uh, nothing personal, Hails, but you know that's not really my bag," I said.

Hailey rolled her eyes as she took another bite of her usual lunch: white rice with salt and butter (yes, it's kind of gross and, yes, Hailey's mother would not be happy if she knew that's what she ate most days). She said, "You just want to go to one of those old-fashioned Jane Austen novel movies or talky-talky movies you like. I just can't sit still for that!"

Kristen and Jenna were used to Hailey's and my battling over details, but everyone knows that underneath it all we're best friends.

"Well, I have to be true to myself," I said, all fake righteous.

"So do I! I just want to kick back, relax, and get scared!"

Everyone laughed, as Hailey had intended, and she smiled a lopsided grin. I didn't want to propose a vote because I knew Jenna and Kristen wanted to see the same movie about old-fashioned times that I did, and it wouldn't be fair to gang up on Hailey. We'd just have to let the movie times decide what we saw and never mind accounting for people's interests.

"Oh, and by the way, there will be way more cute boys at my movie than yours!" said Hailey in one last attempt.

"Hmm. You have a point," I had to admit. "But any cute boys in particular?" These three girls all know about my huge crush on Michael.

Hailey's eyes twinkled. "We could invite him!"

"No. It's a girls' night," I said firmly. We'd been planning on this date for weeks. Not that I would really have the nerve to invite him anyway. Or maybe I would. Would that be weird? I realized they were all looking at me. "Anyway, I'm not going to base my activities on Michael Lawrence's interests!" I declared.

"Famous last words!" Hailey laughed.

"Humph," I said. "Let's change the subject. What do you all know about the candidates for school president?"

"Ooh, John Scott is sooo cute!" said Jenna.

"Majorly," agreed Kristen.

"Hails?" I asked.

"He's cute, I guess. But I didn't know we were voting on looks alone," she said.

"That's my girl!" I cheered. "Good answer!"

"Not that I know anything about the other guy," she said.

"Who is the other guy?" asked Kristen.

"Anthony Wright," I said, shrugging a little.

"No, but who *is* he?" asked Jenna.

"Yeah, I know what you mean," I agreed. "Pretty low on the radar."

"Like, invisible." Kristen nodded.

"I've got to write profiles on them for the *Voice*, so I'll know a lot more very soon," I said.

"Need an assistant for the Scott interview?" joked Jenna.

"I already have one!" I declared. And, spotting Michael across the cafeteria, I said, "And he's right there!"

"Old lover boy, himself," teased Hailey. Here are some of the reasons I love Michael: He is tall and in very good shape from being on the football and baseball teams. He has dark hair with bright blue eyes, which is a great combo, and dimples. He is a good dresser—lots of flannel shirts and khakis—but it's not just the way he looks. He also has nice manners, and he's an excellent writer and a talented cook.

Michael and I mostly get along very well, but we sometimes fight, and I hate that. I want him to always like me, and I want for us to always get along, but when things aren't right, I have to stand up for myself and to him, no matter what. It's just the way I am. I might compromise on some things, but I won't change just to make someone like me.

Remembering my responsibilities, I snapped out of my love-struck dream. There was something I needed to grab from the newsroom, and now would be a good time.

"Okay, chicas, I'm off," I said, gathering up my tray and my messenger bag.

"So soon?" said Hailey.

"Yes, but I'll meet you after school," I said. I usually help Hailey with her homework if I have free time. She's dyslexic and she has a school-appointed tutor, but only one or two days a week. I help the rest of the time since she hates reading and writing and I love it.

"Later!" called Kristen and Jenna.

I walked a few steps away and looked up and there was Michael, standing with his lunch tray. "Leaving so soon?" he asked.

Darn it!

"Uh, yes . . . ?" I stammered.

"Can't you stay for a minute?" he asked.

I sighed. I'd love nothing more, but what I needed to do couldn't wait. "I'm sorry. I just can't," I said.

Michael sighed now, too. "Okay. Maybe later?"

"I have to help Hailey with her homework after school," I said. "Can we talk by phone tonight? Or . . . ?" I was hoping he'd ask me to meet him after school again like he did a few weeks ago.

"Sure. Or maybe we can get together tomorrow," he said.

Yesss!

Michael did a U-turn away from where he'd been heading (toward my table!) and scanned the crowd for his guy friends.

"Great," I said. "Sorry to miss you today."

"Yup," he agreed. "Bye."

"Bye."

Parting is such sweet sorrow, as Shakespeare liked to say. *Oh well. Business is business*, I thought, and I headed back to the newsroom.